Contents

Preface

The History Of Mohammed The Languid

The Monkey, The Shark, And The Washerman's Donkey

The Origin Of Cattle

East African Proverbs

The Hare And The Lion

Goso, The Teacher

The Origin Of Death

The Nunda, Eater Of People

The Lion, The Hyena, And The Rabbit

The Sun And The Moon

Sell Dear, Don't Sell Cheap

The One-Handed Girl

The Kites And The Crows

Thunder And The Gods

An Indian Tale

The Ape, The Snake, And The Lion

The Warrior Who Went To God's Country

The Cheat And The Porter

Haamdaanee

Story Of Liongo

The Magician And The Sultan's Son

The Physician's Son And The King Of The Snakes

Historical Notes

About The Editor

ORIGINAL FICTION BY CLIVE GILSON

- Songs of Bliss
- Out of the Walled Garden
- The Mechanic's Curse
- The Insomniac Booth
- A Solitude of Stars

AS EDITOR – *FIRESIDE TALES* – *Part 1, Europe*

- Tales From the Land of Dragons
- Tales From the Land of The Brave
- Tales From the Land of Saints And Scholars
- Tales From the Land of Hope And Glory
- Tales From Lands of Snow and Ice
- Tales From the Viking Isles
- Tales From the Forest Lands
- Tales From the Old Norse
- More Tales About Saints and Scholars
- More Tales About Hope and Glory
- More Tales About Snow and Ice
- Tales From the Land of Rabbits
- Tales Told by Bulls and Wolves
- Tales of Fire and Bronze
- Tales From the Land of the Strigoi
- Tales Told by the Wind Mother
- Tales from Gallia
- Tales from Germania

I have edited Clive Gilson's books for over a decade now – he's prolific and can turn his hand to many genres - poetry, short fiction, contemporary novels, folklore and science fiction – and the common theme is that none of them ever fails to take my breath away. There's something in each story that is either memorably poignant, hauntingly unnerving or sidesplittingly funny.

Lorna Howarth, The Write Factor

Tales From The World's Firesides is a grand project. I've collected thousands of traditional texts as part of other projects, and while many of the original texts are available through channels like Project Gutenberg, some of the narratives can be hard to read for modern audiences, and so the Fireside project was born. Put simply, I collect, collate and adapt traditional tales from around the world and publish them as a modern archive.

This is the second book in *Part 3 – Africa*, following on from the titles in *Parts 1* and *2* covering a host of nations and regions across Europe and North America.

I'm not laying any claim to insight or specialist knowledge, but these collections are born out of my love of story-telling and I hope that you'll share my affection for traditional tales, myths and legends.

Images by Open Clipart Vectors and e-smile from Pixabay

Hadithi Tales

-

Folklore, Fairy Tales and Legends from East Africa

Compiled & Edited by Clive Gilson

Tales from the World's Firesides

Book 2 in Part 3 of the series: Africa

Hadithi Tales,

edited by Clive Gilson, Solitude, Bath, UK

www.clivegilson.com

First published as an eBook in 2021

2nd edition © 2021 Clive Gilson

3rd edition © 2023 Clive Gilson

All rights reserved. No portion of this book may be reproduced in any form without permission from the publisher, except as permitted by United Kingdom copyright law.

This is a work of fiction. Names, characters, places, and incidents either are the products of the author's imagination or are used fictitiously. Any resemblance to actual persons, living or dead, businesses, companies, events, or locales is entirely coincidental.

Printed by IngramSpark

ISBN: 978-1-913500-44-3

EDITOR – *FIRESIDE TALES – Part 2, North America*

- Okaraxta - Tales from The Great Plains
- Tibik-Kìzis – Tales from The Great Lakes & Canada
- Jóhonaa'éí –Tales from America's Southwest
- Qugaaĝix̂ - First Nation Tales from Alaska & The Arctic
- Karahkwa - First Nation Tales from America's Eastern States
- Pot-Likker - Folklore, Fairy Tales, and Settler Stories from America

EDITOR – *FIRESIDE TALES – Part 3, Africa*

- Arokin Tales – Folklore & Fairy Tales from West Africa
- Hadithi Tales – Folklore & Fairy Tales from East Africa
- Inkathaso Tales – Folklore & Fairy Tales from Southern Africa
- Tarubadur Tales – Folklore & Fairy Tales from North Africa
- Elephant And Frog – Folklore from Central Africa

Preface

I've been collecting and telling stories for a couple of decades now, having had several of my own works published in recent years. My particular focus is on short story writing in the realms of magical realities and science fiction fantasies.

I've always drawn heavily on traditional folk and fairy tales, and in so doing have amassed a collection of many thousands of these tales from around the world. It has been one of my long-standing ambitions to gather these stories together and to create a library of tales that tell the stories of places and peoples from the four corners of our world.

One of the main motivations for me in undertaking the project is to collect and tell stories that otherwise might be lost or, at best forgotten. Given that a lot of my sources are from early collectors, particularly covering works produced in the late eighteenth century, throughout the nineteenth century, and in the early years of the twentieth century, I do make every effort to adapt stories for a modern reader. Early collectors had a different world view to many of us today, and often expressed views about race and gender, for example, that we find difficult to reconcile in the early years of the twenty-first century. I try, although with varying degrees of success, to update these stories with sensitivity while trying to stay as true to the original spirit of each story as I can.

I also want to assure readers that I try hard not to comment on or appropriate originating cultures. It is almost certainly true that the early collectors of these tales, with their then prevalent world views, have made assumptions about the originating cultures that have given us these tales. I hope that you'll accept my mission to preserve these tales, however and wherever I find them, as just that. I have, therefore, made sure that every story has a full attribution, covering both the original collector / writer and the collection title that this version has been adapted from, as well as having notes about publishers and other relevant and, I hope, interesting source data. Wherever possible I have added a cultural or indigenous attribution as well, although for some of the tiles, the country-based theme is obvious.

Hadithi Tales includes a range of stories that originate in East Africa. The seemingly simple art of storytelling is incredibly important in African societies. Storytelling helps those societies to understand core elements such as religion, morals, history, purpose social norms. The collective nature of oral storytelling also helps to cement bonds among generations and family groups, and is significant in the way that it helps people to share experiences and ideas. As with so many cultures the storytellers of Eastern Africa recount tales of heroes and ancestors. These heroes and forebears continue to influence the lives of the living in very real ways.

Oral traditions in East Africa cover both prose and verse forms, often portraying mythological or historical characters and can include tales of the trickster character. Storytellers in Africa sometimes use call-and-response techniques to tell their stories. Poetry, often sung, includes narrative epic, occupational verse, ritual verse, and praise poems of rulers and other prominent people. Praise singers, bards sometimes known as "griots", tell their stories with music.

Examples of pre-colonial African literature are numerous. In Ethiopia, there is a substantial literature written in Ge'ez going back at least to the fourth century AD, the best-known work in this tradition being the *Kebra Negast*, or *Book of Kings*. As I mentioned earlier, one popular form of traditional African folktale is the "trickster" story, in which a small animal uses its wits to survive encounters with larger creatures. Examples of animal tricksters include Anansi, a spider in the folklore of the Ashanti people of Ghana, Ijàpá, a tortoise in the Yoruba folklore of Nigeria, and Sungura, a hare found in central and East African folklore.

In general terms Africa has a hugely rich storytelling heritage. From Timbuktu alone, there are an estimated 300,000 or more manuscripts tucked away in various libraries and private collections, mostly written in Arabic but some in native languages such as Fula and Songhai. Many were written at the famous University of Timbuktu. The material covers a wide array of topics, including astronomy, poetry, law, history, faith, politics, and philosophy.

Swahili literature similarly, draws inspiration from Islamic teachings but developed under indigenous circumstances. One of the most renowned and earliest pieces of Swahili literature being *Utendi wa Tambuka* or *The Story of Tambuka*.

Traditional African religions have also played a key part in forming the African tradition, including belief in higher and lower gods, sometimes including a supreme creator or force. There is a strong sense of belief in spirits, the veneration of the dead, the use of magic, and in traditional African medicine.

Animism is one of the core concepts of traditional African religions, including the worship of tutelary deities, nature worship, ancestor worship and the belief in an afterlife. While some religions adopted a pantheistic worldview, most follow a polytheistic system with various gods, spirits and other supernatural beings. Traditional African religions also have elements of fetishism, shamanism and veneration of relics.

Traditional African medicine is also directly linked to traditional African religions. According to Clemmont E. Vontress, the various religious traditions of Africa are united by a basic Animism. According to him, the belief in spirits and ancestors is the most important element of African religions. Gods were either self-created or evolved from spirits or ancestors which got worshiped by the people.

The wonderous thing about such a rich heritage, and such a long history of finding compelling ways to interpret the world, is that it creates a massive melting pot of full of ideas. Just a few of those ideas are what we have here in this small collection. As ever it has been a delight to discover and work with these stories. I hope you enjoy them.

Clive,

Bath, 2023

The History Of Mohammed The Languid

This story has been edited and adapted from Edward Steere's Swahili Tales, originally published in 1870 by Bell and Daldy, York Street, Covent Garden, London.

It was in the time of the Caliph, the Prince of the Faithful, Haroun al Rashid, when he sat in his court with his Vizirs. And he saw a young slave come in.

And the slave said, "My mistress, the Lady Zubeydeh, sends her compliments. She has made a crown to be worn, but has fallen short of one jewel. Find her a jewel, a large one."

The Caliph looked in his chests, and searched, but all without finding one as large as she wanted. And he said, "Bring me the crown, that I may look at it."

And the slave brought him the crown, which was made of jewels only.

The Caliph showed his Vizirs the crown, and told them, "I want a jewel fit for the top of the crown."

And so it was that each man went out and went to his house to seek for the jewel the Caliph wanted, and each one searched without finding it. What they had were too small to serve for the top of the crown. So, the Caliph went into the town to the merchants, to seek for a jewel large enough, without finding one.

A certain man spoke, and said to the Caliph, "No jewel that will do is to be found here in the district of Bagdad. Perhaps in the district of Bussorah, there is a certain man, a youth named Mohammed the Languid, and there such a jewel will be found."

The Caliph called his Vizir, Mesroor Sayafi. And he told him, "Take a letter, and journey and go to Bussorah, to the governor, Mohammed Zabidi." This was the Caliph's governor in the district of Bussorah.

And Mesroor Sayafi had the letter given him, and was accompanied by a great host, and travelled by the way of the desert, and went to Bussorah. And they entered the district of Bussorah, and arrived at the house of the governor, Mohammed Zabidi.

And Mesroor Sayafi took out the letter and gave it to the governor, who read it. And when he had read it, he invited Mesroor Sayafi into his house, and prepared a great feast for him, and they went in and ate food. And when they had done, Mesroor Sayafi said to him, "My order that was given me was to give you the letter, and when you had read it, for us to go to Mohammed the Languid. And now set forth, and let us go."

So, they set out, and were attended, and went to Mohammed the Languid. And the Vizir, Mesroor Sayafi, took out the letter that came from Haroun al Rashid. And Mohammed the Languid received it with both his hands, and opened it reverentially, and read the letter which came from the Caliph.

And when he had read it, he said, "Come into my house."

Mesroor Sayafi said, "I have no business to go into your house. I was told to give you the letter, and that when you had read it we should make our journey and go, for the Caliph told me, 'Do not stay, give him the letter and come on your way, and let him come with you.'"

And when Mohammed the Languid heard that, he said, "I hear and obey, but I pray you drink a cup of coffee."

Mesroor Sayafi said, "I was not ordered to drink coffee with you."

Mohammed the Languid then said, "You must drink my coffee." And he besought Mesroor Sayafi, and he consented perforce, and he went within his house, and went up-stairs to the reception room. And Mohammed the Languid invited him in, and he entered within, and sat down.

And when he had sat down, there was brought to him a purse of five hundred denars. And Mohammed said, "I beg of you enter the bath, for you have been harassed many days in the journey coming by the desert, and you must be tired, so, I beg of you, enter the bath."

Well, Mesroor Sayafi arose and entered the bath, and the water which was in the bath was scented with roses, that was the kind of water that was in it. And he entered and bathed. And eunuch slaves came and rubbed him with silken towels. And when he had finished, he came out and he was given clothes to dry off the water, and each garment was of silk and gold thread. And he dried off the water. And when he took the drying clothes off, he was brought a packet of other clothes, clothes better than those for drying off the water, and he put them on. And the others were folded up and put with the purse which had been given before. And he went into the reception room and sat down.

And when he had sat down, he lifted up his eyes and looked at the reception room, its furniture, and what was spread on its floor. And he found it very marvellous, and thought in his heart, "Even the Caliph's chamber is not furnished in this way."

And water was brought and Mohammed the Languid washed Mesroor Sayafi, and the governor, Mohammed Zabidi, and all that were there in the reception room. And when they had washed, they saw young slaves enter with food, and they came and laid it out, and they ate. And when they had eaten, Mesroor Sayafi thought, "These viands are such as are not in the universe."

And he was given a sleeping chamber. And he entered his chamber which was prepared for his sleeping, and there came girls wearing exquisite dresses, each one with a musical instrument, and they entered and played their instruments and sang, that they might lull him, and others danced, and made verses in his praise. And he fell asleep, and slept the midday sleep.

And when he awoke, people were sitting ready at the door waiting for him, to go with him to the bath. And he went to the bath and put off his clothes, and they were folded up and put with the former ones, and he went into the bath, and its condition was just as before, and better. Then when he went out from the bath he was given clothes to dry off the water. And when he had dried off the water, he put off those clothes of silk and gold thread. And other clothes were brought him, to go out into the reception room in, and all the clothes were of price. And he put them on and went out.

And when he went out, food was ready, and they went in and ate food. Afterwards they conversed together till night came on, and another chamber was prepared for him. And he went to lie down. And he looked at that chamber, and the furniture that was in it, and its utensils, and it surpassed the chamber in which he lay down at noon. And he slept until the morning.

And Mesroor Sayafi awoke, and people came and took him, and went with him to the bath. And when he came out, he was given other clothes to dry off the water, and afterwards other clothes were brought him, and he put them on. And those he had worn before were folded up, and put away, and every time clothes were brought him, a purse of five hundred denars was also brought to him.

And he went out, and went and ate food. And when they had eaten, he said to Mohammed the Languid, "I have no directions to stay two days, and today is the second, so make your journey and let us go."

But Mohammed the Languid said, "Wait for me till after today, for I want mules to carry my presents which I wish to take to the Caliph."

And Mesroor Sayafi said, "I give you leave for today." And he was transacting his business all that day. And that day the Vizir Mesroor Sayafi had only to rest until sunset. And he entered the bath. And when he came out, clothes were brought to him as before, and he put them on. And all the clothes he took off were folded up and put into a chest, with a purse of five hundred denars. And these clothes and that money were for Mesroor Sayafi himself.

And they waited till the morning, and made their journey. And four hundred mules were brought, and these mules were to carry Mohammed the Languid's things. And they loaded them. And he ordered his two mules to be got ready, with saddles of gold, and bits of gold, and reins of silk. One Mohammed the Languid mounted himself, and one the Vizir, Mesroor Sayafi mounted. And the governor, Mohammed Zabidi, and they went on their journey, journeying to go to the Caliph, in the land of Bagdad. And they set out a great host. And they went along the road.

And when the sun set they got ready their tents and slept. And the tent of Mohammed the Languid, his tent was of silk, and its poles of aloes wood, and they slept, he and the Vizir, Mesroor Sayafi.

In the morning they awoke, and they brought out their food and their drink, and they ate and drank. After that, their beasts were saddled and they mounted. And so it was, when the sun set they slept, and when the night was over they went on. And in the course of that journey, the Vizir Mesroor Sayafi pondered in his heart, and said, "When I reach the Caliph, I will speak to him, to ask this man how he got himself these great riches. I remember his father, he was a cupper at a public bath."

And they went till they reached the Caliph, and made their salutations before the Caliph. And the Caliph was sitting there with his Vizirs. And he welcomed him. And the Languid one fell down at the feet of the Caliph, and said to him, "I ask pardon of you, I have a matter I wish to tell you."

And the Caliph said, "Say on."

Then Mohammed the Languid lifted his face, and looked upward. And he moved his lips, and the top of the house opened, and there came out, as it were, palaces, and gardens, and trees in the gardens, and the leaves of those trees were pearls, and their fruit coral.

And the Caliph was excessively astonished. And he asked him, "Where did you get this wealth? And we only remember you as Mohammed the Languid, and your father was a cupper at the baths. How then did it happen that you got into such circumstances?"

And he answered and said, "If you so order me, I will give you my story, and all these I have not brought you through fear, but I looked upon these as suitable only for you, the king. If then you wish me to give you my story, I will tell it you."

And the king gave him the order, and said, "Tell your story."

And Mohammed the Languid said, "At first when I was young, and when my father died, I was very lazy, so that my mother even fed me. And even when I lay down, I could not turn on the other side, but my mother must come and turn me over. And so it was, my mother used to go and beg, and when she got anything she gave me food. And I remained in this state fifteen years in idleness.

"Till one day my mother went and begged, and got five dirhems, and she came to me there in the house where I was lying, and told me, 'Today I have gone begging, and have got these five dirhems, so take these five dirhems and carry them to Sheikh Abalmathfár. The sheikh is going on a voyage to the land of China. So take these five dirhems and carry them to him. Perhaps where he is going he will buy you some merchandise, so that you may get profit here, for the sheikh is one of the devout men. He loves the poor, so get up and take him these five dirhems.'

"And I answered her, 'I cannot go, my mother, and don't talk to me any more about it.'

"And she said, 'If you don't choose to go, I will just cast you off. I will not give you food, and I will not give you water, nor if you are lying in the sun will I take you out of it. I will leave you to die in your hunger.' And she swore it to me by an oath. And I felt that I should die.

"And I said, 'If you must, then put my sandals ready for me.' And she put my sandals by me. And I said, 'Put them on my feet,' and she put them on. And I said, 'Give me my kanzu.' And she brought it me. And I said, 'Put it on me.' And she gave me a cloth to throw over my shoulder. And I said, 'Give me my staff to lean upon, that I may prop myself with it.' And she put it ready for me. And I said to her, 'Take me up then, that I may stand,' and she took me up. And I said, 'Keep behind and push me, that I may get forward.' And so things were, she pushing me and I lifting one foot at a time, till we reached the shore. And we looked for the Sheikh Abalmathfár. He was putting his goods on board.

"When he saw me, he was astonished, and said, 'What has happened today, that you have got to the shore here?'

"And I gave him my five dirhems, and I said, 'This is my deposit, take them for me where you are going, and buy me some merchandise. This is the business which I came to the shore for.' And the Sheikh Abalmathfár received them.

"And I got myself back to my house, and my condition was just the same, lying down and being fed, and having water given to me to drink.

"And the Sheikh set out, and went his way to the land of China. And they did their trading, and then set out, and went two days' journey. And he forgot my dirhems and had bought me nothing. And he remembered them after two days. And he told his companions, the merchants, 'We must go back, I have forgotten the trust of Mohammed the Languid.'

"And the merchants, his companions, answered and said to him, 'Will you go back for the sake of five dirhems, when we have put so many goods on board the ship?'

"And he said, 'If you will not go back, let each one of you make up for him something certain.' And the merchants consented.

"So they came on their journey and proceeded till they reached an island. And that island was called the island of Sunudi, that was its name. And they landed there, in order to go and rest from the troubles of the sea, and they walked about in the town.

"The Sheikh to whom I had given my deposit passed where there were shops, and saw monkeys tied up, and there was one little one which had all its hair pulled off, and its companions beat it. So when the sheikh saw it, he felt compassion for it, and asked for it from the owner, and bought it with my five dirhems. And the sheikh's idea was to bring it to me to play with, for he knew that I was a man without employment.

"And they set out and came on their way to a second island. And that island was called the island of Sodani, for the inhabitants and their companions eat the flesh of men. And when they saw the ship arrive, they went on board and bound the people who were in it, and some they slaughtered, and ate their flesh. And the Sheikh Abalmathfár was left, with two of his kinsmen, and half the crew. And they were bound, to be killed in the morning.

"But when night was come, the monkey arose and unbound itself first, and then unbound the Sheikh Abalmathfár, and then unbound his kinsmen who were left, until it had unbound them all. When the Sheikh saw that they were unbound, they fled and went away to their ship, and they found it still sound, for it was not yet broken up, and they hoisted their sail and fled. And they went over the sea on their journey home.

"And the people who were in the ship used to dive for pearls. And when the monkey saw the people diving for pearls, it plunged in with them. And the Sheikh said, 'I have lost all the luck of that poor man.' But when the people returned, it too returned with them. And it had brought pearls, and its pearls were better than other people's. And it threw them down at the feet of its Master.

"Then he said to the company, 'Since we should not have escaped, had it not been for this monkey, let each one then give twelve hundred denars, and let us take them to its Master as each man's ransom for his life.'

"And they gave them, and Sheikh Abalmathfár collected them, and put with them the pearls that the monkey had got. And the profits of my five dirhems be put in chests and locked them, and wrote on them the mark of Mohammed the Languid.

"So they journeyed until they reached the country of Bussorah, and they fired their cannons and landed.

"My mother heard that Sheikh Abalmathfár was come, and she came and told me, 'Go out and go and see Sheikh Abalmathfár, and give him the hand of safety.'

"And I told her, 'I cannot go, come and take me up.' "And she took me up, and put on my shoes, and my clothes. Then I told her, 'Give me my stick,' and she gave me my stick. And I said to her, 'Keep behind and push me.' And she kept behind and pushed me, and I lifted up one foot, and she pushed me, and I lifted one foot till we arrived.

"And I met with him and gave him my hand, and he asked after my state. And then he told me, 'Your deposit will come to you in the house.' And when we had met, we set out again, and my mother pushed me until we arrived at our house. And I reached it and got back to my place and lay down.

"In a little while I saw a man come in, and he came and gave me a monkey. And he said, 'With the Sheikh Abalmathfár's compliments.'

And I took the monkey and let him go, and the man who had brought the monkey went out.

"And I called my mother and showed it to her, and said, 'The Sheikh Abalmathfár has brought me something great. Here at home ten monkeys are sold for a dirhem, and he for five dirhems has brought me just one.'

"I had not yet had time to finish saying these words to my mother, when I heard a man at the door calling Hodi! And I said, 'Come in.' And he came in with some keys, and gave me the keys, and I saw porters behind him, and they came in and brought some wonderfully big chests. And he said to me, 'Those are the keys of these chests.'

"And I asked him, 'Why are these chests brought to me?'

"And he said, 'These are your deposit which you gave to Sheikh Abalmathfár to go and buy you merchandise.'

"And I said, 'The Sheikh Abalmathfár had no call to make game of me, who am a poor man. I am a youth before him, and he is a full-grown man before me. He has no call then to make game of me. What was it that I gave him that he should send me these chests? I gave him five dirhems, and the price of the five dirhems is this monkey, which he has brought me. He has no call then to make a jest of me, a poor man.'

"And he who brought the deposit, the chests, said to me, 'He is not making game of you, by Allah, he is not a man to make a jest of you, and he will come himself directly.'

"We had not yet finished talking in this way, when at once I heard, Hodi! And I saw it was the Sheikh Abalmathfár, and I arose of myself and sat up and welcomed him.

"And he sat down, and explained to me his news, from beginning to the end, what had occurred to them from their setting out. And he told me, 'These chests are your profit, and this monkey is the chief of your possessions.' And he begged my forgiveness heartily, and said, 'I am not the man to make a jest of you,' and we took leave of one another, and he went out and went away.

"And we opened a chest and looked, and saw great wealth. And my mother said to me, 'You were idle, you saw nothing, but now Almighty God has given you good luck. Get up then and look for a house that is good, and live in it.'

"So I got up and went and looked for a house, and bought a good house, and bought furniture for the house, and bought slaves for the house, girls, home-born slaves and Abyssinians. And I put them in my house, and everything that was wanted for the house, I bought and put into it. And I bought merchandise and set up a shop.

"And I sat myself in the shop, and my ape sat with me. But in the morning the ape got up and went away, and did not return until the evening, and when it came it brought a bag in its mouth, and it came where I was, and put it before me, and I took hold of the bag and opened it, and saw that it had gold inside, and I poured out the gold, and counted five hundred pieces, and I laid them out and put them away, and waited until the morning. And when I ate, it came and we used to eat together, and I remained in this state, the ape going out in the morning and coming back and producing a bag. And many days passed.

"Then one day at night, I was lying down in my chamber, when the monkey came to me and gave me a salutation, and I answered it. But my heart was troubled, and I was much afraid, because of finding an ape speak. And it said to me, 'Mohammed, be not afraid, as for me,

Almighty God has ordered for me to be an ape, but I am not an ape, I am a Jin of the Marids. Almighty God has ordered for me to be a bringer of good fortune to you, to take you out of poverty, and on your part have no fear. I have a matter I wish to tell you. You used to be one of the poorest, with nothing before and nothing behind. Almighty God made me turn into an ape for your sake, to be the cause of your getting wealth. And now the wealth you have is not completed, for you have no wife. I have got you a wife then, I want to marry you, and if you get this wife you will yourself be at rest, and you will get an increase of wealth.'

"And I asked, 'Who is this wife?'

"And he said, 'Tomorrow in the morning adorn yourself, and put on your best clothes, and let your mule be harnessed with its golden harness, and take with you slave lads of the best from among your slaves, and go to the grass market. Go on as far as the seat of such a one, and you will see the Shereef wearing the garments of a devotee. Go up to him and salute him, and explain to him your news of wanting a wife, of coming to ask in marriage his daughter. He will say to you, 'You have neither root nor branches.' Tell him, 'My root is a thousand denars, and my branches are a thousand denars.' Then tell him all you want, and then give him root and branches, and he will consent, but he will want from you much wealth. What he asks of you, whatever it may be, give him. Don't be stingy, and when the marriage is completed you will repay yourself all the wealth you have laid out and more. And we bade each other good-night, and I slept.

"And when it was light I did as he had told me. And I adorned myself, and my slaves, and my mule, and mounted and went to the market and saw the Shereef and saluted him, and he replied to me. And I said to him, 'Attend,' and I explained to him my news, and he answered me in the words the ape had said. And he said to me, 'You have neither root nor branches.' And I gave him two thousand denars, a thousand for the root and a thousand for the branches. And he consented, and gave me his contract.

"And he said to me, 'A thousand denars is the dowry, and a thousand denars the clothes, and a thousand denars my turban.' And I gave him five thousand denars, and I took out a thousand denars and gave to the bystanders, and I was married. When the marriage was finished I went and told the ape that my marriage was finished.

"And he said to me, 'Your circumstances will be prosperous to you, and I ask about the hour for your going into the house, I have news which I wish to come and tell you.' And I went and inquired about the hour for going into the house, and then I told him, 'I have it.'

"So he said to me, 'The night that you enter the house as you pass the first door, look into the court. You will see a door to the left. There is a ring on the door and in the ring a key. Open and go in. Inside you will see a large chest filling up the room, on the chest there is a pot, and on the pot a brass basin, and in the basin water, and on the left hand side of it there is a red cock, and on the right hand side there is a knife inscribed with a charm. Then take the knife and kill the cock over the chest, and when you have killed it, pour out the water in the basin, and wash the knife. And so when you have completed these directions you will see the chest open, and inside it you will see a treasure, and this treasure the Shereef himself does not know of, and when you have got it you will be at peace. For Almighty God has made me an ape, to come and be the bringer of luck to you. And you yourself will dwell in peace, and I shall go my way. But you must do things in this way, and if you do not, you will not find good, but only evil.'

"And I said, 'I will do as you have told me.'

"And I went and entered the house, and did as I had been directed to do. And as I opened the door, I heard the girl, the Shereef's daughter, my wife, whom I had married, say, 'The Jin has carried me off.' And when I had gone in, and come out again, and went to my wife's room, she was not there, the Jin had carried her off. So my state was like that of a madman.

"And the Shereef, her father, got the news, and came into the house directly, and came weeping and beating himself with his fists, and rending his clothes. And when he reached me there, he said, 'This it was that he wanted, for I found long ago that the Jin wanted to steal away my daughter from me, and I bound him by these charms, which you have dissolved, and those were medicines which bound him, so that he was turned into an ape, and you have come and loosed him, to lose me my daughter. And so now you had better get out of my sight, for I loved my daughter, and am in bitterness about her, yet I do not wish to harm you.'

"And when he said that to me, I saw that so it was. And I arose, and went to my house, and sat thinking and considering, and I felt the house was not the place for me, and I went out to go and look for my wife. And I went without knowing where I ought to go, and I pressed on the road, and went through a forest.

"And I saw two snakes - one white and one black. And the black one came with its mouth open, chasing the white one. And I arose, and struck the black snake, and killed it. The white one went on, and departed. And it went. And then I saw it returning with three white snakes like itself. And they took hold of the black snake, and cut it up into little bits, and threw them away. And they said to me, 'Your courtesy will not be lost.'

"And they asked me, 'Are you not Mohammed the Languid?' And I said, 'I am the languid one.' And they said to me again, 'Your courtesy will not be lost. We know what it is that has banished you from your home. The cause is the Shereef's daughter, and that Marid wished long ago to carry off the woman. And he was no ape, he is a Jin, and as to what he told you about there being a treasure, there was no treasure, they were the bonds that bound him, and he was changed into an ape by the Shereef. And now,' they said to me, 'Please God, you shall get your wife.'

"And they went and returned with a man exceedingly and wonderfully large. And they asked him, 'Do you know such a one?' And that such a one was the Marid that had been an ape. And he said, 'I know him, and now he has changed and become as he was at first, and he has got a wife. He has carried her off and now he has gone to the city of Nuhás. He found the world no place for him.'

"Then they had told him, 'Carry this, your Master, and go with him to the city of Nuhás, where his wife is.' And he said, 'I hear.' So they took him, 'Stoop down,' and he stooped down, and they took me and mounted me upon him. And they took me, 'This is a Marid, so while you are upon him do not invoke the name of Almighty God, for if you invoke the name of Almighty God he will melt away, for he is a Marid.' And I said, 'I will make no invocation.'

"And he said to me, 'Hold yourself well upon me.' And I held on tightly. When I had got hold, he flew and went up with me, I being upon him. And he rose, till from the world where I was as I looked to the earth I saw it no more, I saw the air only. So we went and heard the praises of the angels in heaven, and he went up furiously.

"Then as we went up, I saw a youth of most fair form, with a turban made of a green shawl, carrying a fiery missile. And he called to me by my name, 'Mohammed the Languid!' When he called me, I answered him. And he said to me, 'Invoke the name of Almighty God, or if you do not invoke it, I will strike you with a missile.' And I invoked it.

"As I invoked it the Jin let go of me, and I went off his back. Immediately the youth, when he let go of me, struck him with the missile which he carried in his hand, and he melted away like lead.

"So I was coming on my way till I reached the earth. And I fell into the sea. As I fell I saw a fishing vessel. When they saw me, they came and picked me up, and took me on board their vessel. And they took out some fish for me, and broiled them for me, and I ate. And when I had eaten I found myself a little better. And it was so they spoke with me in their language, but we did not understand one another. And they took me and went with me to their king. And their king knew how to speak Arabic, and the country itself was one of the Indian countries.

"So the king talked with me in the Arabic language, and asked my news, from where I came and how I was going, till I was picked up in the sea. So I gave him the news which I had. The king called his Vizir, and took me and gave me to the Vizir, and told him, 'Find him a place with you, and treat him well, till he recovers his health.'

"So I went and followed him. And I went on, and he gave me a good house, and good sleeping accommodation, and good food, and every good thing he did to me.

"And I remained the days I remained with him. And at the house where I lived there was a garden, and I sat one day and opened the window which faced towards the garden, and I looked, and the garden pleased me exceedingly. And I saw a stream of water in it. And I longed to go and bathe in the stream. And I went down, and got into the water and bathed. And then I followed the stream, and it took me out of the town.

"And when I looked up I did not know where I was, or where I was going, and I was like a man struck with idiocy. Then all at once I saw a man on horseback coming towards where I was. And he called me by my name. And he said to me, 'Your courtesy is not lost.' And he asked me, 'Do you know me?'

"And I said, 'I do not.'

"And he said, 'I am that white snake's brother, and now I am come to complete our business.' And he called me, and said to me, 'Come, let us mount the horse.' And we both got on the horse and went on.

"And he said to me, 'Now we are near the city of Nuhás.' And I knew not where I was, and I knew not where I was going. I knew not before and I knew not behind, I was a mere person. And we went, and arrived at a place where there was a mountain with a river passing under it. So we dismounted there on the mountain. When I had dismounted I looked for him, but saw him no more.

"So I returned to just my first plight, and waited so a little while. And I heard someone salute me, and I replied to him. And he asked me, 'Do you know me?'

"And I said, 'I do not.'

"And he said to me, 'I am the white snake's brother. There are three of us, each one has done what he could for you, and so I have come to do what I can for you.' And he said to me, 'We are near the city of Nuhás, we have reached it, that is it which you see there.'

"And I said, 'I see it. How shall I get in there?'

"And he took out a sword and gave it me, and said to me, 'Carry this sword.' And the sword was all written over with charms.

"And I took hold of the sword, and I asked him, 'Where is the path to enter in by? That is the city of Nuhás, where no one man can open the gate, nor two, nor three, and the gate is fastened. Where shall I pass in?'

"And he said, 'Follow the stream of water, the stream goes into the city of Nuhás.'

"And I followed the stream and carried my sword in my hand. And I followed the stream until I entered into the city. And as I entered I saw marvellous things. I saw every species of things. I saw those that I knew, and those I knew not. And I went with my sword in my hand, and entered into the city, and walked about in the city. And I saw them, but they did not see me, because of my sword which was inscribed with charms.

"And I wandered round till I saw a woman, my wife. When I saw her, immediately I recognised her, and she recognised me, and I came near to her, and we met and asked the news of one another. And I asked her, 'Who brought you here?'

"And she said, 'It was the ape brought me here. When you had finished doing your work, I saw a man, and he carried me away. Then we stayed not anywhere but here. And wherever he wished to stay it did not suit him, except here, for here no mortal man has any desire to reach this place. So now he has come and put me here. And now he is gone on a journey, and here he only comes on his days. And now, do not be afraid, since you have arrived here and you and I have met, we shall go to our home also.'

"And so she explained to me her news. And she told me, 'All the commands of the Jins in this city of Nuhás are his, he has them. And he has works prepared to bind the Jins. Now then be going.' And she gave me directions. 'You will see an iron bar, it has a ring, and there is an incense pot and there is incense. Take the incense, and put it in the censer, and read while it is fuming, and take the ring, and strike the ring with the iron bar. So the Jins will appear to you of every form, each one in anxiety about himself. And when they come, they will say to you, 'We are your slaves, and our command is yours. Order us what you will, we will do it for you. So when they are come, the ordering is yours. What you wish to do to the ape is then up to you.'

"And these words my wife explained to me. And I arose, and went quickly where the iron bar was, and I did as she had told me. And when I had finished striking the bar, at once I saw beings appear to me, some with one eye, some with one arm, some with one leg, and of every form they appeared to me.

"And they said, 'What matter is it you desire? We are your slaves, and the ordering is yours. Say what you desire.'

"And I said to them, 'Where is the Marid who came here with a wife? It was he who was changed into an ape.'

"And they said, 'He is not here, for he is gone on a journey, but it is the second month since he went on his journey, and this is his time for coming.'

"And I said to them, 'Quick! Bind him and bring him.' At once I saw him brought before me, and his hands behind him. And I asked him, 'Are you he that carried off that lady?'

"And he said, 'It was I.'

"So I said to him, 'As the Shereef turned you into an ape and cast you out upon the world, so I will put you in a bottle of copper, and will cast you into the sea.'

Then I took him and put him into a bottle of copper, and carried him to the damsel, and we cast him into the sea. So I ordered the Jins to carry away every choice thing and every rarity. And myself and my wife, we sat upon a couch, with the bar, and the incense-pot and its incense, and everything that pleased me. And I ordered the Jins to carry us.

"And the Jins carried us until we reached the city of Bussorah, and put us inside my house. And I called my father-in-law, the Shereef, in the morning, and he came with my mother, and my relations, and those I loved. And they came, and we met joyfully, talking and laughing. And we made a fresh kind of marriage, and we made a great wedding with joy, and the damsel's father rejoiced exceedingly. And so we dwelt in joy, talking and laughing.

"And as for these things, say not that I prepared them for you through fear, but I felt that these things did not become me, and so I thought I had better give them to you. You are the Caliph, and a great man, and I am a little man."

And the Caliph said to him, "Thanks. Please, stay with us here. Do not go again to Bussorah."

And people were chosen to go to Bussorah, to go and remove his goods. And they came with them to the country of Baghdad, and he dwelt in peace and perfect satisfaction.

The Monkey, The Shark, And The Washerman's Donkey

This story has been edited and adapted from George W. Bateman's Zanzibar Tales, Told by Natives of the East Coast of Africa, first published in 1901 by A. C. McClurg and Company in Chicago. The original stories were translated from the original Swahili and illustrated by Walter Bobbett.

Once upon a time Kee'ma, the monkey, and Pa'pa, the shark, became great friends.

The monkey lived in an immense mkooyoo tree which grew by the margin of the sea, half of its branches being over the water and half over the land.

Every morning, when the monkey was breakfasting on the kooyoo nuts, the shark would put in an appearance under the tree and call out, "Throw me some food, my friend", with which request the monkey complied most willingly.

This continued for many months, until one day Pa'pa said, "Kee'ma, you have done me many kindnesses. I would like you to go with me to my home, that I may repay you."

"How can I go?" said the monkey, "We land beasts cannot go about in the water."

"Don't trouble yourself about that," replied the shark, "I will carry you. Not a drop of water shall get to you."

"Oh, all right, then," said Mr. Kee'ma, "let's go."

When they had gone about half-way the shark stopped, and said, "You are my friend. I will tell you the truth."

"Why, what is there to tell?" asked the monkey, with surprise.

"Well, you see, the fact is that our Sultan is very sick, and we have been told that the only medicine that will do him any good is a monkey's heart."

"Well," exclaimed Kee'ma, "you were very foolish not to tell me that before we started!"

"How so?" asked Pa'pa.

But the monkey was busy thinking up some means of saving himself, and made no reply.

"Well?" said the shark, anxiously, "why don't you speak?"

"Oh, I've nothing to say now. It's too late. But if you had told me this before we started, I might have brought my heart with me."

"What? Haven't you carried your heart here?"

"Huh!" ejaculated Kee'ma, "Don't you know about us? When we go out we leave our hearts in the trees, and go about with only our bodies. But I see you don't believe me. You think I'm scared. Come on. Let's go to your home, where you can kill me and search for my heart in vain."

The shark did believe him, though, and exclaimed, "Oh, no. Let's go back and get your heart."

"Indeed, no," protested Kee'ma, "let us go on to your home."

But the shark insisted that they should go back, get the heart, and start afresh.

At last, with great apparent reluctance, the monkey consented, grumbling sulkily at the unnecessary trouble he was being put to.

When they got back to the tree, he climbed up in a great hurry, calling out, "Wait there, Pa'pa, my friend, while I get my heart, and we'll start off properly next time."

When he had got well up among the branches, he sat down and kept quite still.

After waiting what he considered a reasonable length of time, the shark called, "Come along, Kee'ma!" But Kee'ma just kept still and said nothing.

In a little while he called again, "Oh, Kee'ma! Let's be going."

At this the monkey poked his head out from among the upper branches and asked, in great surprise, "Going? Where?"

"To my home, of course."

"Are you mad?" queried Kee'ma.

"Mad? Why, what do you mean?" cried Pa'pa.

"What's the matter with you?" said the monkey. "Do you take me for a washerman's donkey?"

"What peculiarity is there about a washerman's donkey?"

"It is a creature that has neither heart nor ears."

The shark, his curiosity overcoming his haste, thereupon begged to be told the story of the washerman's donkey, which the monkey related as follows, "A washerman owned a donkey, of which he was very fond. One day, however, it ran away, and took up its abode in the forest, where it led a lazy life, and consequently grew very fat.

"At length Soongoo'ra, the hare, by chance passed that way, and saw Poon'da, the donkey.

"Now, the hare is the most cunning of all beasts. If you look at his mouth you will see that he is always talking to himself about everything.

"So when Soongoo'ra saw Poon'da he said to himself, 'My, this donkey is fat!' Then he went and told Simba, the lion.

"As Simba was just recovering from a severe illness, he was still so weak that he could not go hunting. He was consequently pretty hungry.

"Said Mr. Soongoo'ra, 'I'll bring enough meat tomorrow for both of us to have a great feast, but you'll have to do the killing.'

"'All right, good friend,' exclaimed Simba, joyfully, 'you're very kind.'

"So the hare scampered off to the forest, found the donkey, and said to her, in his most courtly manner, 'Miss Poon'da, I am sent to ask your hand in marriage.'

"'By whom?' simpered the donkey.

"'By Simba, the lion.'

"The donkey was greatly elated at this, and exclaimed, 'Let's go at once. This is a first-class offer.'

"They soon arrived at the lion's home, were cordially invited in, and sat down. Soongoo'ra gave Simba a signal with his eyebrow, to the effect that this was the promised feast, and that he would wait outside. Then he said to Poon'da, 'I must leave you for a while to attend to some private business. You stay here and converse with your husband that is to be.'

"As soon as Soongoo'ra got outside, the lion sprang at Poon'da, and they had a great fight. Simba was kicked very hard, and he struck with his claws as well as his weak health would permit him. At last the donkey threw the lion down, and ran away to her home in the forest.

"Shortly after, the hare came back, and called, 'Haya! Simba! Have you got it?'

"'I have not got it,' growled the lion. 'She kicked me and ran away, but I warrant you I made her feel pretty sore, though I'm not strong.'

"'Oh, well,' remarked Soongoo'ra. 'Don't put yourself out of the way about it.'

"Then Soongoo'ra waited many days, until the lion and the donkey were both well and strong, when he said, 'What do you think now, Simba? Shall I bring you your meat?'

"'Ay,' growled the lion, fiercely. 'Bring it to me. I'll tear it in two pieces!'

"So the hare went off to the forest, where the donkey welcomed him and asked the news.

"'You are invited to call again and see your lover,' said Soongoo'ra.

"'Oh, dear!' cried Poon'da. 'That day you took me to him he scratched me awfully. I'm afraid to go near him now.'

"'Ah, pshaw!' said Soongoo'ra. 'That's nothing. That's only Simba's way of caressing.'

"'Oh, well,' said the donkey, 'let's go.'

"So off they started again, but as soon as the lion caught sight of Poon'da he sprang upon her and tore her in two pieces.

"When the hare came up, Simba said to him, 'Take this meat and roast it. As for myself, all I want is the heart and ears.'

"'Thanks,' said Soongoo'ra. Then he went away and roasted the meat in a place where the lion could not see him, and he took the heart and ears and hid them. Then he ate all the meat he needed, and put the rest away.

"Presently the lion came to him and said, 'Bring me the heart and ears.'

"'Where are they?' said the hare.

"'What does this mean?' growled Simba.

"'Why, didn't you know this was a washerman's donkey?'

"'Well, what's that to do with there being no heart or ears?'

"'For goodness' sake, Simba, aren't you old enough to know that if this beast had possessed a heart and ears it wouldn't have come back the second time?'

"Of course the lion had to admit that what Soongoo'ra, the hare, said was true.

"And now," said Kee'ma to the shark, "you want to make a washerman's donkey of me. Get out of there, and go home by yourself. You are not going to get me again, and our friendship is ended. Good-bye, Pa'pa."

The Origin Of Cattle

This story is based on a traditional Maasai folk tale, of which there are many variations. This adaptation is my own simple version based on my reading of a number of those sources.

At the start of the world the Maasai did not have any cattle. After a while God called upon Maasinta, who was the first of the Maasai, and said to him, "I want you to make a large enclosure, and when you have done this, come back and tell me all about it."

Maasinta went and did just this, making everything safe and secure, just as he had been instructed. Then he went back to tell God of all that he had done.

Then God said to him, "Early tomorrow morning, I want you to go and stand against the outside wall of your house and I will give you a gift. I will give you cattle. Now, when you see or hear anything at all do not be surprised or afraid, but do remember to stay very quiet."

So, very early the next morning, Maasinta went to wait outside of the wall of his house. He soon heard peals of deep, rolling thunder, and God released a long leather thong all the way from heaven down to the earth. Cattle walked down this thong from the clouds and right into the enclosure. There were so many cattle walking that the earth shook vigorously and Maasinta's house almost disintegrated.

Maasinta was now gripped with fear, but he did not make any movement or sound. However, while the cattle were still descending from heaven, Dorobo, who was Maasinta's house-mate, woke up from his slumbers and went outside. When he saw the countless droves of cattle coming down the thong, he was so surprised that he shouted, "Ayeeee!", in complete and utter shock.

When God heard this he rolled the thong back up into the heavens, and the cattle stopped descending. God then said to Maasinta, thinking that he was the one who had screamed out, "Don't you want any more cattle? Have you seen enough already? I am shocked. I will never send you any more cattle, so you had better love these cattle in the same way I love you." That is why the Maasai love cattle very much.

Of course, Maasinta was very upset with Dorobo for screaming out and making God cut the thong. He cursed him, saying, "Dorobo, you are the man who cut God's thong! You will remain as poor as you have always been and both you and your children will be my servants until the end of time. You must live off animals in the wild and the milk of my cattle will forever be poison to you."

This is why even now the Dorobo still live in the forest and they never drink milk.

East African Proverbs

These proverbs have been edited and adapted from Edward Steere's Swahili Tales, originally published in 1870 by Bell and Daldy, York Street, Covent Garden, London.

- Hurrying, hurrying, has no blessing.
- The tongue has no bone.
- The destroyer of the country is a child of the country; a stranger does not weigh two hundred-weight.
- A new thing is good, though it be a sore place.
- Running on a roof ends at the edge of it.
- Is not poor work good play?
- Wonder not, children of men, at the things that are in this world.
- If the Pleiades rise in sun, they set in rain; if they rise in rain, they set in sun.
- If a dish is covered, what is in it is hidden.
- There is no grief without a companion.
- Who will dance to a lion's roaring? Patience is the key of consolation.
- Continually, continually, the cord cuts the stone.
- When two elephants struggle it is the grass that suffers.
- Use your clay while it is wet.

- He that is drunk with wine gets sober, he that is drunk with wealth does not.
- What bites is in your own clothes.
- Loud lamentations are not becoming in mourning.
- A sand-fly can get through anything.
- He has fallen into a well.

The Hare And The Lion

This story has been edited and adapted from George W. Bateman's Zanzibar Tales, Told by Natives of the East Coast of Africa, first published in 1901 by A. C. McClurg and Company in Chicago. The original stories were translated from the original Swahili and illustrated by Walter Bobbett.

One day Soongoo'ra, the hare, roaming through the forest in search of food, glanced up through the boughs of a very large calabash tree, and saw that a great hole in the upper part of the trunk was inhabited by bees. He immediately returned to town in search of someone to go with him and help to get the honey.

As he was passing the house of Boo'koo, the big rat, that worthy gentleman invited him in. So he went in, sat down, and remarked, "My father has died, and has left me a hive of honey. I would like you to come and help me to eat it."

Of course Boo'koo jumped at the offer, and he and the hare started off immediately.

When they arrived at the great calabash tree, Soongoo'ra pointed out the bees' nest and said, "Go on, climb up."

So, taking some straw with them, they climbed up to the nest, lit the straw, smoked out the bees, put out the fire, and set to work eating the honey.

In the midst of the feast, who should appear at the foot of the tree but Simba, the lion? Looking up, and seeing them eating, he asked, "Who are you?"

Then Soongoo'ra whispered to Boo'koo, "Hold your tongue. That old fellow is crazy."

But in a very little while Simba roared out angrily, "Who are you, I say? Speak, I tell you!"

This made Boo'koo so scared that he blurted out, "It's only us!"

Upon this the hare said to him, "You just wrap me up in this straw, call to the lion to keep out of the way, and then throw me down. Then you'll see what will happen."

So Boo'koo, the big rat, wrapped Soongoo'ra, the hare, in the straw, and then called to Simba, the lion, "Stand back. I'm going to throw this straw down, and then I'll come down myself."

When Simba stepped back out of the way, Boo'koo threw down the straw, and as it lay on the ground Soongoo'ra crept out and ran away while the lion was looking up.

After waiting a minute or two, Simba roared out, "Well, come down, I say!" and, there being no help for it, the big rat came down. As soon as he was within reach, the lion caught hold of him, and asked, "Who was up there with you?"

"Why," said Boo'koo, "Soongoo'ra, the hare. Didn't you see him when I threw him down?"

"Of course I didn't see him," replied the lion, in an incredulous tone, and, without wasting further time, he ate the big rat, and then searched around for the hare, but could not find him.

Three days later, Soongoo'ra called on his acquaintance, Ko'bay, the tortoise, and said to him, "Let us go and eat some honey."

"Whose honey?" inquired Ko'bay, cautiously.

"My father's," Soongoo'ra replied.

"Oh, all right. I'm with you," said the tortoise, eagerly, and away they went.

When they arrived at the great calabash tree they climbed up with their straw, smoked out the bees, sat down, and began to eat. Just then Mr. Simba, who owned the honey, came out again, and, looking up, inquired, "Who are you, up there?"

Soongoo'ra whispered to Ko'bay, "Keep quiet", but when the lion repeated his question angrily, Ko'bay became suspicious, and said, "I will speak. You told me this honey was yours. Am I right in suspecting that it belongs to Simba?"

So, when the lion asked again, "Who are you?" Ko'bay answered, "It's only us."

The lion said, "Come down, then"

The tortoise answered, "We're coming."

Now, Simba had been keeping an eye open for Soongoo'ra since the day he caught Boo'koo, the big rat, and, suspecting that he was up there with Ko'bay, he said to himself, "I've got him this time, for sure."

Seeing that they were caught again, Soongoo'ra said to the tortoise, "Wrap me up in the straw, tell Simba to stand out of the way, and then throw me down. I'll wait for you below. He can't hurt you, you know."

"All right," said Ko'bay, but while he was wrapping the hare up he said to himself, "This fellow wants to run away, and leave me to bear the lion's anger. He shall get caught first." Therefore, when he had bundled him up, he called out, "Soongoo'ra is coming!" and threw him down.

So Simba caught the hare, and, holding him with his paw, said, "Now, what shall I do with you?"

The hare replied, "It's no use for you to try to eat me. I'm awfully tough."

"What would be the best thing to do with you, then?" asked Simba.

"I think," said Soongoo'ra, "you should take me by the tail, whirl me around, and knock me against the ground. Then you may be able to eat me."

So the lion, being deceived, took him by the tail and whirled him around, but just as he was going to knock him on the ground Soongoo'ra slipped out of his grasp and ran away, and Simba had the mortification of losing him again.

Angry and disappointed, he turned to the tree and called to Ko'bay, "You come down, too."

When the tortoise reached the ground, the lion said, "You're pretty hard. what can I do to make you eatable?"

"Oh, that's easy," laughed Ko'bay, "just put me in the mud and rub my back with your paw until my shell comes off."

Immediately on hearing this, Simba carried Ko'bay to the water, placed him in the mud, and began, as he supposed, to rub his back, but the tortoise had slipped away, and the lion continued rubbing on a piece of rock until his paws were raw. When he glanced down at them he saw they were bleeding, and, realizing that he had again been outwitted, he said, "Well, the hare has done me today, but I'll go hunting now until I find him."

So Simba, the lion, set out immediately in search of Soongoo'ra, the hare, and as he went along he asked everyone he met, "Where is the house of Soongoo'ra?"

But each person he asked answered, "I do not know." For the hare had said to his wife, "Let us remove from this house." Therefore the folks in that neighbourhoods had no knowledge of his whereabouts.

Simba, however, went along, continuing his inquiries, until presently one answered, "That is his house on the top of the mountain."

The lion climbed the mountain, and soon arrived at the place indicated, only to find that there was no one at home. This, however, did not trouble him. On the contrary. He said to himself, "I'll hide myself inside, and when Soongoo'ra and his wife come home I'll eat them both." Then entered the house and lay down, awaiting their arrival.

Pretty soon along came the hare with his wife, not thinking of any danger, but he very soon discovered the marks of the lion's paws on the steep path. Stopping at once, he said to Mrs. Soongoo'ra, "You go back, my dear. Simba, the lion, has passed this way, and I think he must be looking for me."

But she replied, "I will not go back. I will follow you, my husband."

Although greatly pleased at this proof of his wife's affection, Soongoo'ra said firmly, "No, no. You have friends to go to. Go back."

So he persuaded her, and she went back, but he kept on, following the footmarks, and saw, as he had suspected, that they went into his house.

"Ah," he said to himself, "Mr. Lion is inside, is he?"

Then, cautiously going back a little way, he called out, "How d'ye do, house? How d'ye do?" Waiting a moment, he remarked loudly, "Well, this is very strange! Every day, as I pass this place, I say, 'How d'ye do, house?' and the house always answers, 'How d'ye do?' There must be someone inside today."

When the lion heard this he called out, "How d'ye do?"

Then Soongoo'ra burst out laughing, and shouted, "Oho, Mr. Simba! You're inside, and I'll bet you want to eat me, but first tell me where you ever heard of a house talking!"

Upon this the lion, seeing how he had been fooled, replied angrily, "You wait until I get hold of you, that's all."

"Oh, I think you'll have to do the waiting," cried the hare as he ran away with the lion following.

But it was of no use. Soongoo'ra completely tired out old Simba. Exhausted, the lion said to himself, "That rascal has beaten me. I don't want to have anything more to do with him." Then he returned to his home under the great calabash tree.

Goso, The Teacher

This story has been edited and adapted from Edward Steere's Swahili Tales, originally published in 1870 by Bell and Daldy, York Street, Covent Garden, London.

There was a teacher who taught children to read under a calabash tree, and this teacher's name was Goso. And one day a gazelle came and climbed up the calabash tree, and threw down a calabash, and it struck the teacher, and he died. His scholars took their teacher and went and buried him.

When they had finished burying him they said, "Let us go and look for the creature who threw down the calabash which struck our teacher Goso, and when we get him let us kill him."

Then they said, "It was the south wind that threw down the calabash. It blew, and threw down the calabash, and it struck our teacher, so let us go and look for the south wind, and beat it."

And they took the south wind and beat it. And the south wind said, "I am the south wind. You are beating me. What have I done?"

And they said, "It was you, south wind, who threw down the calabash, and it struck our teacher Goso. You should not do it."

And the south wind said, "If I were the chief, should I be stopped by a mud wall?"

And they went and took the mud wall and beat it. And the mud wall said, "Why do you beat me, what have I done?"

And they said, "You, mud wall, should stop the south wind, but the south wind threw down the calabash, and it struck our teacher Goso. You should have stopped it."

And the mud wall said, "If I were the chief, should I be bored through by the rat?"

And they went and took the rat and beat it.

And the rat said, "Why do you beat me? What have I done?" And they said, "You, the rat, bore a hole through the mud wall, which stops the south wind, and the south wind threw down the calabash, and it struck our teacher Goso. You should not do it."

And the rat said, "If I were the chief, should I be eaten by the cat?"

And they went and looked for the cat, and took it and beat it.

And the cat said, "Why do you beat me? What have I done?"

And they said, "You are the cat which eats the rat, and the rat bores through the mud wall, and the mud wall stops the south wind, and the south wind threw down the calabash, and it struck our teacher Goso. You should eat the rat."

And the cat said, "If I were the chief, should I be tied by a rope?"

And they went and took the rope and beat it.

And the rope said, "I am a rope, you are beating me, what have I done?"

And they said, "You are the rope which ties the cat, and stops the cat from eating the rat, and the rat bores holes through the mud wall, and the mud wall stops the south wind, but the south wind threw down the calabash, and it struck our teacher Goso. You should not do it."

And the rope said, "If I were the chief, should I be cut by a knife?"

And they went and took the knife and beat it.

And the knife said, "Why do you beat me? What have I done?"

And they said, "You are the knife which cuts the rope, and the rope ties the cat and stops the cat from eating the rat, and the rat bores through the mud wall, and the mud wall stops the south wind, and the south wind threw down the calabash, and it struck our teacher Goso. You should have cut the rope." And the knife said, "If I were the chief, should I be consumed by the fire?"

And they went and took the fire and beat it.

And the fire said, "Why do you beat me? What have I done?"

And they said, "You are the fire which consumes the knife, and the knife cuts the cord, and the cord ties the cat, and the cat eats the rat, and the rat bores through the mud wall, and the mud wall stops the south wind, and the south wind threw down the calabash, and it struck our teacher Goso. You should not burn the knife."

And the fire said, "If I were the chief should I be put out by water?"

And they went and took the water and beat it.

And the water said, "Why do you beat me? What have I done?"

And they said, "You are the water which puts out the fire, and the fire consumes the knife so that the knife cannot cut the rope, and the rope ties the cat and stops the cat from eating the rat, and the rat bores through the mud wall, and the mud wall stops the south wind, and the south wind threw down the calabash, and it struck our teacher Goso. You should put the fire out."

And the water said, "If I were the chief should I be drunk by the ox?"

And they went and took the ox and beat it.

And the ox said, "Why do you beat me? What have I done?"

And they said, "You are the ox which drinks the water, so that the water cannot put out the fire, and so the fire consumes the knife, and the knife cannot cut the rope, and the rope ties the cat so that the cat cannot eat the rat, and so the rat bores through the mud wall, and the mud wall stops the south wind, and the south wind threw down the calabash, and it struck our teacher Goso. You should not drink the water."

And the ox said, "If I, the ox, were the chief, should I be stuck to by a tick."

And they went and took the tick and beat it.

And the tick said, "Why do you beat me? What have I done?"

And they said, "You are the tick which sticks to the ox, and makes the ox drink the water, for the water puts out the fire, and the fire consumes the knife, so the knife cannot cut the rope, and the rope ties the cat, and the cat cannot eat the rat, so the rat bores through the mud wall, and the mud wall stops the south wind, and the south wind threw down the calabash, and it struck our teacher Goso. You should not stick to the ox."

And the tick said, "If I were the chief should I be eaten by the gazelle?"

And they went and searched for the gazelle, and when they found it they took it and beat it.

And the gazelle said, "I am the gazelle, why do you beat me? What have I done?"

And they said, "You are the gazelle which should eat the tick, but the tick sticks to the ox, and so the ox drinks the water that should out the fire, so the fire consumes the knife, and the knife cannot cut the rope, so the rope ties the cat, and the cat cannot eat the rat, and so the rat bores through the mud wall, and the mud wall stops the south wind, and the south wind threw down the calabash, and it struck our teacher Goso. You should eat the tick."

The gazelle held its tongue, without saying a word.

And they said, "This is the one that threw down the calabash, and it struck our teacher Goso, and we will kill him."

And they took the gazelle and they killed it.

The Origin Of Death

This story is based on a traditional Maasai folk tale, of which there are many variations. This adaptation is my own simple version based on my reading of a number of those sources.

When the world was young there was no death. Leeyio was the first man brought to the earth by Naiteru-kop. Naiteru-Kop then called Leeyio and said to him, "When a man dies and you dispose of the corpse, you must remember to say, 'man die and come back again, moon die, and remain away'."

Many months went by before anyone died. When, in the end, a child did die, Leeyio was summoned to dispose of the body. When he took the corpse outside, he made a mistake and said, "Moon die and come back again, man die and stay away."

So after that no one ever survived death.

A few more months went by and Leeyio's own child went missing. Leeyio took his child's body outside and said, "Moon die and remain away, man die and come back again."

When Naiteru-kop heard this he said, "You are too late now. Your mistake with your neighbour's child allowed death to be born."

That is how death came about, and that is why up to this day when a man dies he does not return, but when the moon dies, it always comes back again.

The Nunda, Eater Of People

This story has been edited and adapted from Andrew Lang's The All Sorts Of Stories Book, first published in 1911 by Longmans, Green and Company of London and New York. Lang's story was taken from the original Swahili Tales by Edward Steere, LL.D.

Once upon a time there lived a Sultan who loved his garden dearly, and planted it with trees and flowers and fruits from all parts of the world. He went to see them three times every day, first at seven o'clock, when he got up, then at three, and lastly at half-past five. There was no plant and no vegetable which escaped his eye, but he lingered longest of all before his one date tree.

Now the Sultan had seven sons. Six of them he was proud of, for they were strong and manly, but the youngest he disliked, for he spent all his time among the women of the house. The Sultan had talked to him, and he paid no heed, and he had beaten him, and he paid no heed, and he had tied him up, and he paid no heed, till at last his father grew tired of trying to make him change his ways, and let him alone.

Time passed, and one day the Sultan, to his great joy, saw signs of fruit on his date tree. And he told his Vizir, "My date tree is bearing." He told the officers, "My date tree is bearing." He told the judges, "My date tree is bearing." He told all the rich men of the town.

He waited patiently for some days till the dates were nearly ripe, and then he called his six sons, and said, "One of you must watch the date tree till the dates are ripe, for if it is not watched the slaves will steal them, and I shall not have any for another year."

And the eldest son answered, "I will go, father," and he went.

The first thing the youth did was to summon his slaves, and bid them beat drums all night under the date tree, for he feared to fall asleep. So the slaves beat the drums, and the young man danced till four o'clock, and then it grew so cold he could dance no longer, and one of the slaves said to him, "It is getting light and the tree is safe. Lie down, Master, and go to sleep."

So he lay down and slept, and his slaves slept likewise.

A few minutes went by, and a bird flew down from a neighbouring thicket, and ate all the dates, without leaving a single one. And when the tree was stripped bare, the bird went as it had come. Soon after, one of the slaves woke up and looked for the dates, but there were no dates to see. Then he ran to the young man and shook him, saying, "Your father set you to watch the tree, and you have not watched, and the dates have all been eaten by a bird."

The lad jumped up and ran to the tree to see for himself, but there was not a date anywhere. And he cried aloud, "What am I to say to my father? Shall I tell him that the dates have been stolen, or that a great rain fell and a great storm blew? But he will send me to gather them up and bring them to him, and there are none to bring! Shall I tell him that Bedouins drove me away, and when I returned there were no dates? And he will answer, "You had slaves, did they not fight with the Bedouins?" It is the truth that will be best, and that will I tell him."

Then he went straight to his father, and found him sitting in his verandah with his five sons round him, and the lad bowed his head.

"Give me the news from the garden," said the Sultan.

And the youth answered, "The dates have all been eaten by some bird, there is not one left."

The Sultan was silent for a moment. Then he asked, "Where were you when the bird came?:

The lad answered, "I watched the date tree till the cocks were crowing and it was getting light. Then I lay down for a little, and I slept. When I woke a slave was standing over me, and he said, "There is not one date left on the tree!" And I went to the date tree, and saw it was true, and that is what I have to tell you."

And the Sultan replied, "A son like you is only good for eating and sleeping. I have no use for you. Go your way, and when my date tree bears again, I will send another son. Perhaps he will watch better."

So he waited many months, till the tree was covered with more dates than any tree had ever borne before. When they were near ripening he sent one of his sons to the garden, saying, "My son, I am longing to taste those dates. Go and watch over them, for today's sun will bring them to perfection."

And the lad answered, "My father, I am going now, and tomorrow, when the sun has passed the hour of seven, bid a slave come and gather the dates."

"Good," said the Sultan.

The youth went to the tree, and lay down and slept. And about midnight he arose to look at the tree, and the dates were all there - beautiful dates, swinging in bunches.

"Ah, my father will have a feast, indeed," thought he. "What a fool my brother was not to take more heed! Now he is in disgrace, and we know him no more. Well, I will watch till the bird comes. I should like to see what manner of bird it is."

And he sat and read till the cocks crew and it grew light, and the dates were still on the tree.

"Oh my father will have his dates. They are all safe now," he thought to himself. "I will make myself comfortable against this tree," and he leaned against the trunk, and sleep came on him, and the bird flew down and ate all the dates.

When the sun rose, the head-man came and looked for the dates, and there were no dates. And he woke the young man, and said to him, "Look at the tree."

And the young man looked, and there were no dates. And his ears were stopped, and his legs trembled, and his tongue grew heavy at the thought of the Sultan. His slave became frightened as he looked at him, and asked, "My Master, what is it?"

He answered, "I have no pain anywhere, but I am ill everywhere. My whole body is well, and my whole body is sick. I fear my father, for did I not say to him, "Tomorrow at seven you shall taste the dates." And he will drive me away, as he drove away my brother! I will go away myself, before he sends me."

Then he got up and took a road that led straight past the palace, but he had not walked many steps before he met a man carrying a large silver dish, covered with a white cloth to cover the dates.

And the young man said, "The dates are not ripe yet. You must return tomorrow."

And the slave went with him to the palace, where the Sultan was sitting with his four sons.

"Good greeting, Master!" said the youth.

And the Sultan answered, "Have you seen the man I sent?"

"I have, Master, but the dates are not yet ripe."

But the Sultan did not believe his words, and said, "This second year I have eaten no dates, because of my sons. Go your ways, you are my son no longer!"

And the Sultan looked at the four sons that were left him, and promised rich gifts to whichever of them would bring him the dates from the tree. But year by year passed, and he never got them. One son tried to keep himself awake with playing cards, another mounted a horse and rode round and round the tree, while the two others, whom their father as a last hope sent together, lit bonfires. But whatever they did, the result was always the same. Towards dawn they fell asleep, and the bird ate the dates on the tree.

The sixth year had come, and the dates on the tree were thicker than ever. And the head-man went to the palace and told the Sultan what he had seen. But the Sultan only shook his head, and said sadly, "What is that to me? I have had seven sons, yet for five years a bird has devoured my dates, and this year it will be the same as ever."

Now the youngest son was sitting in the kitchen, as was his custom, when he heard his father say those words. And he rose up, and went to his father, and knelt before him. "Father, this year you shall eat dates," cried he. "And on the tree are five great bunches, and each bunch I will give to a separate nation, for the nations in the town are five. This time, I will watch the date tree myself." But his father and his mother laughed heartily, and thought his words idle talk.

One day, news was brought to the Sultan that the dates were ripe, and he ordered one of his men to go and watch the tree. His son, who happened to be standing by, heard the order, and he said, "How is it that you have bidden a man to watch the tree, when I, your son, am left?"

And his father answered, "Ah, six were of no use, and where they failed, will you succeed?"

But the boy replied, "Have patience today, and let me go, and tomorrow you shall see whether I bring you dates or not."

"Let the child go, Master," said his wife, "perhaps we shall eat the dates - or perhaps we shall not - but let him go."

And the Sultan answered, "I do not refuse to let him go, but my heart distrusts him. His brothers all promised fair, and what did they do?"

But the boy entreated, saying, "Father, if you and I and mother be alive tomorrow, you shall eat the dates."

"Go then," said his father.

When the boy reached the garden, he told the slaves to leave him, and to return home themselves and sleep. When he was alone, he laid himself down and slept fast till one o'clock, when he arose, and sat opposite the date tree. Then he took some Indian corn out of one fold of his dress, and some sandy grit out of another.

And he chewed the corn till he felt he was growing sleepy, and then he put some grit into his mouth, and that kept him awake till the bird came.

It looked about at first without seeing him, and whispering to itself, "There is no one here," fluttered lightly on to the tree and stretched out his beak for the dates. Then the boy stole softly up, and caught it by the wing.

The bird turned and flew quickly away, but the boy never let go, not even when they soared high into the air.

"Son of Adam," the bird said when the tops of the mountains looked small below them, "if you fall, you will be dead long before you reach the ground, so go your way, and let me go mine."

But the boy answered, "Wherever you go, I will go with you. You cannot get rid of me."

"I did not eat your dates," persisted the bird, "and the day is dawning. Leave me to go my way."

But again the boy answered him, "My six brothers are hateful to my father because you came and stole the dates, and today my father shall see you, and my brothers shall see you, and all the people of the town, great and small, shall see you. And my father's heart will rejoice."

"Well, if you will not leave me, I will throw you off," said the bird.

So it flew up higher still - so high that the earth shone like one of the other stars.

"How much of you will be left if you fall from here?" asked the bird.

"If I die, I die," said the boy, "but I will not leave you."

And the bird saw it was no use talking, and went down to the earth again.

"Here you are at home, so let me go my way," it begged once more, "or at least make a covenant with me."

"What covenant?" said the boy.

"Save me from the sun," replied the bird, "and I will save you from rain."

"How can you do that, and how can I tell if I can trust you?"

"Pull a feather from my tail, and put it in the fire, and if you want me I will come to you, wherever I am."

And the boy answered, "Well, I agree. Go your way."

"Farewell, my friend. When you call me, if it is from the depths of the sea, I will come."

The lad watched the bird out of sight, then he went straight to the date tree. And when he saw the dates his heart was glad, and his body felt stronger and his eyes brighter than before. And he laughed out loud with joy, and said to himself, "This is MY luck, mine, Sit-in-the-kitchen! Farewell, date tree, I am going to lie down. What ate you will eat you no more."

The sun was high in the sky before the head-man, whose business it was, came to look at the date tree, expecting to find it stripped of all its fruit, but when he saw the dates so thick that they almost hid the leaves he ran back to his house, and beat a big drum till everybody came running, and even the little children wanted to know what had happened.

"What is it? What is it, head-man?" cried they.

"Ah, it is not a son that the Master has, but a lion! This day Sit-in-the-kitchen has uncovered his face before his father!"

"But how, head-man?"

"Today the people may eat the dates."

"Is it true, head-man?"

"Oh yes, it is true, but let him sleep till each man has brought forth a present. He who has fowls, let him take fowls, he who has a goat, let him take a goat, he who has rice, let him take rice." And the people did as he had said.

Then they took the drum, and went to the tree where the boy lay sleeping.

And they picked him up, and carried him away, with horns and clarinets and drums, with clappings of hands and shrieks of joy, straight to his father's house.

When his father heard the noise and saw the baskets made of green leaves, brimming over with dates, and his son borne high on the necks of slaves, his heart leaped, and he said to himself, "Today at last I shall eat dates." And he called his wife to see what her son had done, and ordered his soldiers to take the boy and bring him to his father.

"What news, my son?" said he.

"News? I have no news, except that if you will open your mouth you shall see what dates taste like." And he plucked a date, and put it into his father's mouth.

"Ah! You are indeed my son," cried the Sultan. "You do not take after those fools, those good-for-nothings. But, tell me, what did you do with the bird, for it was you, and you only who watched for it?"

"Yes, it was I who watched for it and who saw it. And it will not come again, neither for its life, nor for your life, nor for the lives of your children."

"Oh, once I had six sons, and now I have only one. It is you, whom I called a fool, who have given me the dates. As for the others, I want none of them."

But his wife rose up and went to him, and said, "Master, do not, I pray you, reject them," and she entreated long, till the Sultan granted her prayer, for she loved the six elder ones more than her last one.

So they all lived quietly at home, till the Sultan's cat went and caught a calf. And the owner of the calf went and told the Sultan, but he answered, "The cat is mine, and the calf mine," and the man dared not complain further.

Two days after, the cat caught a cow, and the Sultan was told, "Master, the cat has caught a cow," but he only said, "It was my cow and my cat."

And the cat waited a few days, and then it caught a donkey, and they told the Sultan, "Master, the cat has caught a donkey," and he said, "My cat and my donkey." Next it was a horse, and after that a camel, and when the Sultan was told he said, "You don't like this cat, and want me to kill it. And I shall not kill it. Let it eat the camel. Let it even eat a man."

And it waited till the next day, and caught someone's child. And the Sultan was told, "The cat has caught a child." And he said, "The cat is mine and the child mine." Then it caught a grown-up man.

After that the cat left the town and took up its abode in a thicket near the road. So if anyone passed, going for water, it devoured him. If it saw a cow going to feed, it devoured him. If it saw a goat, it devoured him. Whatever went along that road the cat caught and ate.

Then the people went to the Sultan in a body, and told him of all the misdeeds of that cat. But he answered as before, "The cat is mine and the people are mine." And no man dared kill the cat, which grew bolder and bolder, and at last came into the town to look for its prey.

One day, the Sultan said to his six sons, "I am going into the country, to see how the wheat is growing, and you shall come with me." They went on merrily along the road, till they came to a thicket, when out sprang the cat, and killed three of the sons.

"The cat! The cat!" shrieked the soldiers who were with him. And this time the Sultan said, "Seek for it and kill it. It is no longer a cat, but a demon!"

And the soldiers answered him, "Did we not tell you, Master, what the cat was doing, and did you not say, 'My cat and my people'?"

And he answered, "True, I said it."

Now the youngest son had not gone with the rest, but had stayed at home with his mother, and when he heard that his brothers had been killed by the cat he said, "Let me go, that it may slay me also." His mother entreated him not to leave her, but he would not listen, and he took his sword and a spear and some rice cakes, and went after the cat, which by this time had run off to a great distance.

The lad spent many days hunting the cat, which now bore the name of 'The Nunda, eater of people', but though he killed many wild animals he saw no trace of the enemy he was hunting for. There was no beast, however fierce, that he was afraid of, till at last his father and mother begged him to give up the chase after the Nunda.

But he answered, "What I have said, I cannot take back. If I am to die, then I die, but every day I must go and look for the Nunda."

And again his father offered him what he would, even the crown itself, but the boy would hear nothing, and went on his way.

Many times his slaves came and told him, "We have seen footprints, and today we shall behold the Nunda." But the footprints never turned out to be those of the Nunda. They wandered far through deserts and through forests, and at length came to the foot of a great hill. And something in the boy's soul whispered that here was the end of all their seeking, and today they would find the Nunda.

But before they began to climb the mountain the boy ordered his slaves to cook some rice, and they rubbed the stick to make a fire, and when the fire was kindled they cooked the rice and ate it. Then they began their climb.

Suddenly, when they had almost reached the top, a slave who was on in front cried, "Master! Master!" And the boy pushed on to where the slave stood, and the slave said, "Cast your eyes down to the foot of the mountain."

The boy looked, and his soul told him it was the Nunda. And he crept down with his spear in his hand, and then he stopped and gazed below him.

"This MUST be the real Nunda," thought he. "My mother told me its ears were small, and this one's are small. She told me it was broad and not long, and this is broad and not long. She told me it had spots like a civet-cat, and this has spots like a civet-cat."

Then he left the Nunda lying asleep at the foot of the mountain, and went back to his slaves.

"We will feast today," he said, "make cakes of batter, and bring water," and they ate and drank. And when they had finished he bade them hide the rest of the food in the thicket, so that if they slew the

Nunda they might return and eat and sleep before going back to the town. And the slaves did as he bade them.

It was now afternoon, and the lad said, "It is time we went after the Nunda." And they went till they reached the bottom and came to a great forest which lay between them and the Nunda.

Here the lad stopped, and ordered every slave that wore two cloths to cast one away and tuck up the other between his legs. "For," said he, "the wood is not a little one. Perhaps we may be caught by the thorns, or perhaps we may have to run before the Nunda, and the cloth might bind our legs, and cause us to fall before it."

And they answered, "Good, Master," and did as he bade them. Then they crawled on their hands and knees to where the Nunda lay asleep.

Noiselessly they crept along till they were quite close to it, then, at a sign from the boy, they threw their spears. The Nunda did not stir, the spears had done their work, but a great fear seized them all, and they ran away and climbed the mountain.

The sun was setting when they reached the top, and glad they were to take out the fruit and the cakes and the water which they had hidden away, and sit down and rest themselves. And after they had eaten and were filled, they lay down and slept till morning.

When the dawn broke they rose up and cooked more rice, and drank more water. After that they walked all-round the back of the mountain to the place where they had left the Nunda, and they saw it stretched out where they had found it, stiff and dead. And they took it up and carried it back to the town, singing as they went, "He has killed the Nunda, the eater of people."

And when his father heard the news, and that his son was come, and was bringing the Nunda with him, he felt that the man did not dwell on the earth whose joy was greater than his. And the people bowed down to the boy and gave him presents, and loved him, because he had delivered them from the bondage of fear, and had slain the Nunda.

So he lay down and slept, and his slaves slept likewise.

A few minutes went by, and a bird flew down from a neighbouring thicket, and ate all the dates, without leaving a single one. And when the tree was stripped bare, the bird went as it had come. Soon after, one of the slaves woke up and looked for the dates, but there were no dates to see. Then he ran to the young man and shook him, saying, "Your father set you to watch the tree, and you have not watched, and the dates have all been eaten by a bird."

The lad jumped up and ran to the tree to see for himself, but there was not a date anywhere. And he cried aloud, "What am I to say to my father? Shall I tell him that the dates have been stolen, or that a great rain fell and a great storm blew? But he will send me to gather them up and bring them to him, and there are none to bring! Shall I tell him that Bedouins drove me away, and when I returned there were no dates? And he will answer, "You had slaves, did they not fight with the Bedouins?" It is the truth that will be best, and that will I tell him."

Then he went straight to his father, and found him sitting in his verandah with his five sons round him, and the lad bowed his head.

"Give me the news from the garden," said the Sultan.

And the youth answered, "The dates have all been eaten by some bird. there is not one left."

The Sultan was silent for a moment. Then he asked, "Where were you when the bird came?:

The lad answered, "I watched the date tree till the cocks were crowing and it was getting light. Then I lay down for a little, and I slept. When I woke a slave was standing over me, and he said, "There is not one date left on the tree!" And I went to the date tree, and saw it was true, and that is what I have to tell you."

And the Sultan replied, "A son like you is only good for eating and sleeping. I have no use for you. Go your way, and when my date tree bears again, I will send another son. Perhaps he will watch better."

So he waited many months, till the tree was covered with more dates than any tree had ever borne before. When they were near ripening he sent one of his sons to the garden, saying, "My son, I am longing to taste those dates. Go and watch over them, for today's sun will bring them to perfection."

And the lad answered, "My father, I am going now, and tomorrow, when the sun has passed the hour of seven, bid a slave come and gather the dates."

"Good," said the Sultan.

The youth went to the tree, and lay down and slept. And about midnight he arose to look at the tree, and the dates were all there - beautiful dates, swinging in bunches.

"Ah, my father will have a feast, indeed," thought he. "What a fool my brother was not to take more heed! Now he is in disgrace, and we know him no more. Well, I will watch till the bird comes. I should like to see what manner of bird it is."

And he sat and read till the cocks crew and it grew light, and the dates were still on the tree.

"Oh my father will have his dates. They are all safe now," he thought to himself. "I will make myself comfortable against this tree," and he leaned against the trunk, and sleep came on him, and the bird flew down and ate all the dates.

When the sun rose, the head-man came and looked for the dates, and there were no dates. And he woke the young man, and said to him, "Look at the tree."

And the young man looked, and there were no dates. And his ears were stopped, and his legs trembled, and his tongue grew heavy at the thought of the Sultan. His slave became frightened as he looked at him, and asked, "My Master, what is it?"

He answered, "I have no pain anywhere, but I am ill everywhere. My whole body is well, and my whole body is sick. I fear my father, for did I not say to him, "Tomorrow at seven you shall taste the dates." And he will drive me away, as he drove away my brother! I will go away myself, before he sends me."

Then he got up and took a road that led straight past the palace, but he had not walked many steps before he met a man carrying a large silver dish, covered with a white cloth to cover the dates.

And the young man said, "The dates are not ripe yet. You must return tomorrow."

And the slave went with him to the palace, where the Sultan was sitting with his four sons.

"Good greeting, Master!" said the youth.

And the Sultan answered, "Have you seen the man I sent?"

"I have, Master, but the dates are not yet ripe."

But the Sultan did not believe his words, and said, "This second year I have eaten no dates, because of my sons. Go your ways, you are my son no longer!"

And the Sultan looked at the four sons that were left him, and promised rich gifts to whichever of them would bring him the dates from the tree. But year by year passed, and he never got them. One son tried to keep himself awake with playing cards, another mounted a horse and rode round and round the tree, while the two others, whom their father as a last hope sent together, lit bonfires. But whatever they did, the result was always the same. Towards dawn they fell asleep, and the bird ate the dates on the tree.

The sixth year had come, and the dates on the tree were thicker than ever. And the head-man went to the palace and told the Sultan what he had seen. But the Sultan only shook his head, and said sadly, "What is that to me? I have had seven sons, yet for five years a bird has devoured my dates, and this year it will be the same as ever."

Now the youngest son was sitting in the kitchen, as was his custom, when he heard his father say those words. And he rose up, and went to his father, and knelt before him. "Father, this year you shall eat dates," cried he. "And on the tree are five great bunches, and each bunch I will give to a separate nation, for the nations in the town are five. This time, I will watch the date tree myself." But his father and his mother laughed heartily, and thought his words idle talk.

One day, news was brought to the Sultan that the dates were ripe, and he ordered one of his men to go and watch the tree. His son, who happened to be standing by, heard the order, and he said, "How is it that you have bidden a man to watch the tree, when I, your son, am left?"

And his father answered, "Ah, six were of no use, and where they failed, will you succeed?"

But the boy replied, "Have patience today, and let me go, and tomorrow you shall see whether I bring you dates or not."

"Let the child go, Master," said his wife, "perhaps we shall eat the dates - or perhaps we shall not - but let him go."

And the Sultan answered, "I do not refuse to let him go, but my heart distrusts him. His brothers all promised fair, and what did they do?"

But the boy entreated, saying, "Father, if you and I and mother be alive tomorrow, you shall eat the dates."

"Go then," said his father.

When the boy reached the garden, he told the slaves to leave him, and to return home themselves and sleep. When he was alone, he laid himself down and slept fast till one o'clock, when he arose, and sat opposite the date tree. Then he took some Indian corn out of one fold of his dress, and some sandy grit out of another.

And he chewed the corn till he felt he was growing sleepy, and then he put some grit into his mouth, and that kept him awake till the bird came.

It looked about at first without seeing him, and whispering to itself, "There is no one here," fluttered lightly on to the tree and stretched out his beak for the dates. Then the boy stole softly up, and caught it by the wing.

The bird turned and flew quickly away, but the boy never let go, not even when they soared high into the air.

"Son of Adam," the bird said when the tops of the mountains looked small below them, "if you fall, you will be dead long before you reach the ground, so go your way, and let me go mine."

But the boy answered, "Wherever you go, I will go with you. You cannot get rid of me."

"I did not eat your dates," persisted the bird, "and the day is dawning. Leave me to go my way."

But again the boy answered him, "My six brothers are hateful to my father because you came and stole the dates, and today my father shall see you, and my brothers shall see you, and all the people of the town, great and small, shall see you. And my father's heart will rejoice."

"Well, if you will not leave me, I will throw you off," said the bird.

So it flew up higher still - so high that the earth shone like one of the other stars.

"How much of you will be left if you fall from here?" asked the bird.

"If I die, I die," said the boy, "but I will not leave you."

And the bird saw it was no use talking, and went down to the earth again.

"Here you are at home, so let me go my way," it begged once more, "or at least make a covenant with me."

"What covenant?" said the boy.

"Save me from the sun," replied the bird, "and I will save you from rain."

"How can you do that, and how can I tell if I can trust you?"

"Pull a feather from my tail, and put it in the fire, and if you want me I will come to you, wherever I am."

And the boy answered, "Well, I agree, go your way."

"Farewell, my friend. When you call me, if it is from the depths of the sea, I will come."

The lad watched the bird out of sight, then he went straight to the date tree. And when he saw the dates his heart was glad, and his body felt stronger and his eyes brighter than before. And he laughed out loud with joy, and said to himself, "This is MY luck, mine, Sit-in-the-kitchen! Farewell, date tree, I am going to lie down. What ate you will eat you no more."

The sun was high in the sky before the head-man, whose business it was, came to look at the date tree, expecting to find it stripped of all its fruit, but when he saw the dates so thick that they almost hid the leaves he ran back to his house, and beat a big drum till everybody came running, and even the little children wanted to know what had happened.

"What is it? What is it, head-man?" cried they.

"Ah, it is not a son that the Master has, but a lion! This day Sit-in-the-kitchen has uncovered his face before his father!"

"But how, head-man?"

"Today the people may eat the dates."

"Is it true, head-man?"

"Oh yes, it is true, but let him sleep till each man has brought forth a present. He who has fowls, let him take fowls. He who has a goat, let him take a goat. He who has rice, let him take rice." And the people did as he had said.

Then they took the drum, and went to the tree where the boy lay sleeping.

And they picked him up, and carried him away, with horns and clarinets and drums, with clappings of hands and shrieks of joy, straight to his father's house.

When his father heard the noise and saw the baskets made of green leaves, brimming over with dates, and his son borne high on the necks of slaves, his heart leaped, and he said to himself "Today at last I shall eat dates." And he called his wife to see what her son had done, and ordered his soldiers to take the boy and bring him to his father.

"What news, my son?" said he.

"News? I have no news, except that if you will open your mouth you shall see what dates taste like." And he plucked a date, and put it into his father's mouth.

"Ah! You are indeed my son," cried the Sultan. "You do not take after those fools, those good-for-nothings. But, tell me, what did you do with the bird, for it was you, and you only who watched for it?"

"Yes, it was I who watched for it and who saw it. And it will not come again, neither for its life, nor for your life, nor for the lives of your children."

"Oh, once I had six sons, and now I have only one. It is you, whom I called a fool, who have given me the dates, as for the others, I want none of them."

But his wife rose up and went to him, and said, "Master, do not, I pray you, reject them," and she entreated long, till the Sultan granted her prayer, for she loved the six elder ones more than her last one.

So they all lived quietly at home, till the Sultan's cat went and caught a calf. And the owner of the calf went and told the Sultan, but he answered, "The cat is mine, and the calf mine," and the man dared not complain further.

Two days after, the cat caught a cow, and the Sultan was told, "Master, the cat has caught a cow," but he only said, "It was my cow and my cat."

And the cat waited a few days, and then it caught a donkey, and they told the Sultan, "Master, the cat has caught a donkey," and he said, "My cat and my donkey." Next it was a horse, and after that a camel, and when the Sultan was told he said, "You don't like this cat, and want me to kill it. And I shall not kill it. Let it eat the camel. Let it even eat a man."

And it waited till the next day, and caught someone's child. And the Sultan was told, "The cat has caught a child." And he said, "The cat is mine and the child mine." Then it caught a grown-up man.

After that the cat left the town and took up its abode in a thicket near the road. So if anyone passed, going for water, it devoured him. If it saw a cow going to feed, it devoured him. If it saw a goat, it devoured him. Whatever went along that road the cat caught and ate.

Then the people went to the Sultan in a body, and told him of all the misdeeds of that cat. But he answered as before, "The cat is mine and the people are mine." And no man dared kill the cat, which grew bolder and bolder, and at last came into the town to look for its prey.

One day, the Sultan said to his six sons, "I am going into the country, to see how the wheat is growing, and you shall come with me." They went on merrily along the road, till they came to a thicket, when out sprang the cat, and killed three of the sons.

"The cat! The cat!" shrieked the soldiers who were with him. And this time the Sultan said,

"Seek for it and kill it. It is no longer a cat, but a demon!"

And the soldiers answered him, "Did we not tell you, Master, what the cat was doing, and did you not say, "My cat and my people"?"

And he answered, "True, I said it."

Now the youngest son had not gone with the rest, but had stayed at home with his mother, and when he heard that his brothers had been killed by the cat he said, "Let me go, that it may slay me also." His mother entreated him not to leave her, but he would not listen, and he took his sword and a spear and some rice cakes, and went after the cat, which by this time had run off to a great distance.

The lad spent many days hunting the cat, which now bore the name of "The Nunda, eater of people," but though he killed many wild animals he saw no trace of the enemy he was hunting for. There was no beast, however fierce, that he was afraid of, till at last his father and mother begged him to give up the chase after the Nunda.

But he answered, "What I have said, I cannot take back. If I am to die, then I die, but every day I must go and seek for the Nunda."

And again his father offered him what he would, even the crown itself, but the boy would hear nothing, and went on his way.

Many times his slaves came and told him, "We have seen footprints, and today we shall behold the Nunda." But the footprints never turned out to be those of the Nunda. They wandered far through deserts and through forests, and at length came to the foot of a great hill. And something in the boy's soul whispered that here was the end of all their seeking, and today they would find the Nunda.

But before they began to climb the mountain the boy ordered his slaves to cook some rice, and they rubbed the stick to make a fire, and when the fire was kindled they cooked the rice and ate it. Then they began their climb.

Suddenly, when they had almost reached the top, a slave who was on in front cried:

"Master! Master!" And the boy pushed on to where the slave stood, and the slave said,

"Cast your eyes down to the foot of the mountain." And the boy looked, and his soul told him it was the Nunda.

And he crept down with his spear in his hand, and then he stopped and gazed below him.

"This MUST be the real Nunda," thought he. "My mother told me its ears were small, and this one's are small. She told me it was broad and not long, and this is broad and not long. She told me it had spots like a civet-cat, and this has spots like a civet-cat."

Then he left the Nunda lying asleep at the foot of the mountain, and went back to his slaves.

"We will feast today," he said, "make cakes of batter, and bring water," and they ate and drank. And when they had finished he bade them hide the rest of the food in the thicket, that if they slew the Nunda they might return and eat and sleep before going back to the town. And the slaves did as he bade them.

It was now afternoon, and the lad said, "It is time we went after the Nunda." And they went till they reached the bottom and came to a great forest which lay between them and the Nunda.

Here the lad stopped, and ordered every slave that wore two cloths to cast one away and tuck up the other between his legs. "For," said he, "the wood is not a little one. Perhaps we may be caught by the thorns, or perhaps we may have to run before the Nunda, and the cloth might bind our legs, and cause us to fall before it."

And they answered, "Good, Master," and did as he bade them. Then they crawled on their hands and knees to where the Nunda lay asleep.

Noiselessly they crept along till they were quite close to it. Then, at a sign from the boy, they threw their spears. The Nunda did not stir. The spears had done their work, but a great fear seized them all, and they ran away and climbed the mountain.

The sun was setting when they reached the top, and glad they were to take out the fruit and the cakes and the water which they had hidden away, and sit down and rest themselves. And after they had eaten and were filled, they lay down and slept till morning.

When the dawn broke they rose up and cooked more rice, and drank more water. After that they walked all-round the back of the mountain to the place where they had left the Nunda, and they saw it stretched out where they had found it, stiff and dead. And they took it up and carried it back to the town, singing as they went, "He has killed the Nunda, the eater of people."

And when his father heard the news, and that his son was come, and was bringing the Nunda with him, he felt that the man did not dwell on the earth whose joy was greater than his. And the people bowed down to the boy and gave him presents, and loved him, because he had delivered them from the bondage of fear, and had slain the Nunda.

The Lion, The Hyena, And The Rabbit

This story has been edited and adapted from George W. Bateman's Zanzibar Tales, Told by Natives of the East Coast of Africa, first published in 1901 by A. C. McClurg and Company in Chicago. The original stories were translated from the original Swahili and illustrated by Walter Bobbett.

Once upon a time Simba, the lion, Feesee, the hyena, and Keeteetee, the rabbit, made up their minds to go in for a little farming. So they went into the country, made a garden, planted all kinds of seeds, and then came home and rested quite a while.

Then, when the time came when their crops should be about ripe and ready for harvesting, they began to say to each other, "Let's go over to the farm, and see how our crops are coming along."

So one morning, early, they started, and, as the garden was a long way off, Keeteetee, the rabbit, made this proposition, "While we are going to the farm, let us not stop on the road, and if anyone does stop, let him be eaten." His companions, not being so cunning as he, and knowing they could outwalk him, readily consented to this arrangement.

Well, off they went, but they had not gone very far when the rabbit stopped.

"Hello!" said Feesee, the hyena, "Keeteetee has stopped. He must be eaten."

"That's the bargain," agreed Simba, the lion.

"Well," said the rabbit, "I happened to be thinking."

"What about?" cried his partners, with great curiosity.

"I'm thinking," said he, with a grave, philosophical air, "about those two stones, one big and one little. The little one does not go up, nor does the big one go down."

The lion and the hyena, having stopped to look at the stones, could only say, "Why, really, it's singular, but it's just as you say," and they all resumed their journey, the rabbit being by this time well rested.

When they had gone some distance the rabbit stopped again.

"Aha!" said Feesee, "Keeteetee has stopped again. Now he must be eaten."

"I rather think so," assented Simba.

"Well," said the rabbit, "I was thinking again."

Their curiosity once more aroused, his comrades begged him to tell them his think.

"Why," said he, "I was thinking this. When people like us put on new coats, where do the old ones go to?"

Both Simba and Feesee, having stopped a moment to consider the matter, exclaimed together, "Well, I wonder!" and the three went on, the rabbit having again had a good rest.

After a little while the hyena, thinking it about time to show off a little of his philosophy, suddenly stopped.

"Here," growled Simba, "this won't do. I guess we'll have to eat you, Feesee."

"Oh, no," said the hyena, "I'm thinking."

"What are you thinking about?" they inquired.

"I'm thinking about nothing at all," said he, imagining himself very smart and witty.

"Ah, pshaw!" cried Keeteetee, "We won't be fooled that way."

So he and Simba ate the hyena.

When they had finished eating their friend, the lion and the rabbit proceeded on their way, and presently came to a place where there was a cave, and here the rabbit stopped.

"H'm!" said Simba, "I'm not so hungry as I was this morning, but I guess I'll have to find room for you, little Keeteetee."

"Oh, I believe not," replied Keeteetee, "I'm thinking again."

"Well," said the lion, "what is it this time?"

Said the rabbit, "I'm thinking about that cave. In olden times our ancestors used to go in here, and go out there, and I think I'll try and follow in their footsteps."

So he went in at one end and out at the other end several times.

Then he said to the lion, "Simba, old fellow, let's see you try to do that," and the lion went into the cave, but he stuck fast, and could neither go forward nor back out.

In a moment Keeteetee was on Simba's back, and began eating him.

After a little time the lion cried, "Oh, brother, be impartial, come and eat some of the front part of me."

But the rabbit replied, "Indeed, I can't come around in front, I'm ashamed to look you in the face."

So, having eaten all he was able to, he left the lion there, and went and became sole owner of the farm and its crops.

The Sun And The Moon

This story is based on a traditional Maasai folk tale, of which there are many variations. This adaptation is my own simple version based on my reading of a number of those sources.

In the earliest of times the sun married the moon. They went about the world for a very long time, with the sun leading and the moon following. As they travelled, the moon would get tired and the sun would carry her for three days every month.

It is said that on the fourth day donkeys can see the moon, but people can only see the moon on the fifth day.

Anyway, one day the moon made a mistake and she was chastised by the sun. But the moon was short-tempered and she fought back. She managed to wound the sun's forehead, while the sun scratched her face and plucked out one of her eyes.

When the sun realised that he was wounded, he was very embarrassed and said to himself, "I am going to shine so hard that people will not be able to look at me." And so he shone so hard that people could not look at him without squinting. That is why the sun shines so brightly.

As for the moon, she did not feel any embarrassment and so she did not have to shine any brighter. Even now, if you look closely at the moon, you will see the wounds that the sun inflicted on her during their fight.

Sell Dear, Don't Sell Cheap

This story has been edited and adapted from Edward Steere's Swahili Tales, originally published in 1870 by Bell and Daldy, York Street, Covent Garden, London.

There was a great and very wealthy merchant, and he was the Sultan's Vizir. And he lived amongst his businesses, and had one son. And the name of that son was Ali. And when his child had reached his five and twentieth year, the father died. And the boy was left with his mother.

And Ali inherited his property, and spent his property very fast. At last Ali had spent everything and was now exceedingly poor. There was no one in that town who would help him, neither friends of his own, nor those of his father. And he was still a young man, and he walked about in the town quite alone.

Everyone who saw Ali used to ask him, "What have you done with your property, Ali, that you have lost it all so quickly? For your father left much wealth, and if you had been wise, you would have had it still."

And Ali said, "He who does not know the meaning of it, will not be told."

And this speech of his was his employment. Throughout the town people knew that Ali, if one asked him, "What have you done with your property?" used to say, "He that does not know the meaning of it, will not be told."

And the words reached the Sultan. And people told the Sultan, "That son of your Vizir, Ali, has gone to ruin, and if people ask him, 'What have you done with your property, Ali, that it is so soon ended? For your late father left you much property. If you had been wise, Ali, his property would have remained yours, for that property was large.' Ali answers, and tells whoever asks him, 'He that does not know the meaning of it, will not be told.'"

And the Sultan said, "Bring Ali to me, that I may ask him whether these words are true which people say, or whether they slander him."

And the cadi said, "Yes, Sultan, the words are true." And he sent a soldier to go and call him to come at the time of the public audience, and that all the people at the Sultan's public audience might come and hear whether the words which Ali said were true or false.

So Ali went and borrowed from a poor man a ragged old kanzu, for there was no one who would trust him with his clothes, and this kanzu Ali only got by entreaties and prostrations.

And so he went to the Sultan's door, and the audience was very full and the Sultan was seated. And the Sultan arose and called him, "Ali!"

And he answered, "Here."

And the Sultan said, "Ali, I have heard say that your property has come to ruin, and that in reply to people who ask you, you say, 'He who does not know the meaning of it, will not be told.'"

And Ali said, "Yes, Master, I made this property into four parts, one part I threw into the sea, one part I put into the fire, one part I lent and shall not be paid, and with the last part I paid a debt and have not yet paid it all."

And the Sultan said, "Ali, sell dear, don't sell cheap."

And Ali said, "All right, sir." And he went out and went his way.

And the Sultan's Vizir arose in the audience and said, "O our lord, I know the meaning of these words."

And the Sultan answered and said to him, "If you know the meaning of these words without asking Ali, and truly know the meaning by your own understanding, I, the Sultan, will give you my Sultanship, and all of my worldly goods, I, the Sultan, will give you as yours. And if you know not the meaning of these words by your own understanding, I shall take all your property. But you must not ask Ali to explain the meaning of his words."

And the Vizir said, "If I know not these words by my own understanding, I, the Vizir, will give you, the Sultan, all of my possessions, except my wife, who shall return to her family, and my head shall be lawful to you, Sultan."

And the Sultan said, "And I will descend from my Sultanship to be your Vizir, I who am Sultan."

And the Vizir arose and went to his house, and bent down and considered, and he went and took books, of which there were a great number in his house. And he opened them to see the meaning of Ali's words, without finding a single page that had Ali's words on it. So he sat thinking and pondering, "I have told the Sultan that I should know these words by my own understanding, and now I have considered and pondered and I do not know their meaning."

And he called, "Juma! Where does that young man Ali live?"

And Juma said, "Which Ali, Master?"

And he said, "That young man who had much property, the son of the late Vizir Hassan, who has ruined himself. Do you not know where he lives? I beg of you to take me, I have a business I want to ask him about. And these words of mine to you, let no one know them. And I will set you free, for the sake of your secrecy."

And Juma said, "All right, all right, I know where he lives. There, away at the end of the town, there is a little lean-to near the shore. There he lives with the one eyed beggar who goes about begging, he is his friend, and that is where he lives, he has no other place."

And the Vizir arose in the night, at twelve o'clock, when everyone was asleep, he and one of his slaves, a confidential slave of his, and they went on till they arrived. And the Vizir tapped at the lean-to and called, "Ali! Ali!" And Ali was afraid and did not answer. And the Vizir said, "Ali!"

And Ali said to his friend, "Wake, wake!"

And the beggar asked him, "What is the matter?"

And Ali said, "There is a man knocking at our shed, and I wonder at night now whether it is a drunken man, or a man coming to steal inside here. But we are beggars, we have nothing. Perhaps the man wants to insult us, and to take our lives. However, I say, let us wait quiet a bit and listen, and if he taps at our door a third time let us answer. Perhaps we may know his voice."

And the beggar said, "How come you to be so silly, Ali? Someone is come in the middle of the night and we don't know where he comes from, and we are not used to having people come tapping at our door. What does this man want, except perhaps he has three things he wants with us, as God has granted me, I think of these three things in my soul, it is as Almighty God pleases."

And Ali said, "What then, my friend, what is the meaning of these three things which you think of in your soul? Tell me, that I may know, that we may both know. Tell me the first."

And the beggar said, "The first, he wants to come stealing, the second, he wants to come and kill us, the third, perhaps he thinks his wife, or his female slave is here. These are what I think in my soul." And then he said, "I know not, my friend, whatsoever comes from God is good."

And Ali said, "If he taps now I will answer him. if he kills me let him kill me. If he leaves me alone, that is well, but I can't help answering him."

And the Vizir tapped, and called him, "Ali!"

And Ali answered, "Here, who are you that come calling me in the night, and in the middle of the night too?"

And the Vizir said, "It is I, I have business with you?"

And Ali said, "I don't know you who are come, Master."

And the Vizir said, "Don't be afraid, I have come to call you for good, and not for harm."

And Ali said, "Master, call me to your house, and wait for me there till the morning."

The Vizir said, "Here where I am, I cannot wait for you even one minute, as you are talking there inside I feel you are delaying. I beg of you, Ali, come outside, and hear the matter I want you for."

And Ali said, "All right, Master, I am putting my ear to the door. Tell me your name, then I shall trust myself to come out, for then I shall know you."

And the Vizir went and said, "It is I, the Sultan's Vizir, I beg of you come out, I have a matter to tell you, and it is a matter of privacy."

"All right, my Master." And Ali went and told his friend the beggar, "I have come to be called by the Sultan's Vizir. He who refuses to be called, refuses what he is called for."

And the beggar said, "Go, my friend, perhaps there is good luck for you."

And as he opened the door Ali saw the Vizir and his slave. And he said, "Master, Masalkhieri."

And the Vizir said, "Thanks, Ali, let us be going and make our way to my house."

And Ali said, "All right, Master."

The Vizir and Ali went together to his house. As the Vizir went up-stairs, it struck one o'clock. And the Vizir called his slave woman, "Mrashi!"

And she answered, "Here."

"Tell the mistress to get food ready quickly, before two o'clock strikes, and then come back."

When Mrashi came back she said, "I am come, Master."

And he said, "Mrashi, unlock the chest and bring a turban cloth, and bring a white embroidered cap, and bring a kanzu of khuzurungi, and bring a loin-cloth with a border, and all these I have fastened together in a parcel with a red handkerchief. Bring them quickly."

And the Vizir arose and said to Ali, "I have called you for good, though I beg of you that no man may know of this business. Keep it to yourself."

And Ali said, "All right, Master. Could I betray your matters, Master?"

And the Vizir said, "I want you, Ali, to give me the meaning of the words you told the Sultan, and the words the Sultan said to you."

And he said, "The Sultan told me, 'Sell dear, don't sell cheap.'"

"Ali, Ali, I beg of you tell me those words. Why will you say to me, 'The Sultan told me, Sell dear, and not cheap'? I will give you my plantation."

And Ali said, "The Sultan told me, 'Sell dear, don't sell cheap?'"

And the Vizir said, "Ali, take all my shops and storerooms that are in the town."

And Ali said, "The Sultan told me, 'Sell dear, don't sell cheap.'"

The Vizir said, "Ali, take all my plantations."

And Ali said, "The Sultan told me, 'Sell dear, don't sell cheap.'"

The Vizir said, "Take all my possessions."

And Ali said, "The Sultan told me, 'Sell dear, don't sell cheap.'"

And the Vizir said, "Take what speaks, and what speaks not, take all of my possessions, and tell me those words."

And Ali said, "The Sultan told me, 'Sell dear, don't sell cheap.'"

And the Vizir arose and said, I will give you all my house that I live in, and all the goods that are in it, except my wife."

And Ali said, "Well then, write me your promise in your own hand."

And the Vizir called Mrashi. And she answered, "Here, Master." And he said, "Bring the pen and ink and paper, from the niche in the wall." And Mrashi went and brought them. The Vizir took hold of the paper and ink, and wrote for Ali, "I have given him all my possessions, which speak and which speak not, even to my house which I myself dwell in, save only my wife, the daughter of a family, who should go to her family home." And the Vizir took the note and gave it to Ali.

"It is now four o'clock, let us go and perform our devotions first, so that when we come back from prayers I may give you the meanings you want."

And they went down-stairs and went to their devotions, and returned from the mosque. And the Vizir said, "Now then, Ali, tell me, for it is getting light."

And Ali said, "The meaning of the saying, 'He who does not know the meaning of it, will not be told,' is this. if I tell a man who has no understanding, even then he will not know it. That is the meaning of telling everyone that asked me, 'He who does not know the meaning of it, will not be told.' And when the Sultan called me, he was not told so, because the Sultan has understanding. And he replied, 'Sell dear, don't sell cheap.' These are your words."

"Well, explain to me the loss of the property."

And Ali said, "I made this property into four parts, one part I put in the sea, one part I set on fire, one part I lent and shall not be paid, with one part I paid a debt which I have not yet done paying."

"Tell me, then, Ali, the meaning of sinking one part in the sea. What is the meaning of that?"

And Ali said to the Vizir, "Forgive me for all that I shall say, and bear with it." And he said, "In the sea is the property that I actually spent in dissipation with women. That property is lost, and I shall not get it again. So then, it is as if I had put it in the sea, for what sinks in the sea, is not to be had again."

"And the meaning of setting one part on fire?"

Ali said, "I ate much, I dressed much, I spent much. That is the meaning of setting it on fire, for it will not return into my hands."

"Tell me as to the third part. What is the meaning of lending, and you will not be repaid?"

And Ali said to the Vizir, "It is as if a man should give his wife a dowry, for it returns not again. So this is the meaning of telling you I lent and shall not be repaid."

And the Vizir said, "As to the fourth part, tell me the meaning of saying you have paid a debt but have not finished paying it."

And Ali said to the Vizir, "It is like a man who has given his mother property, wishing to please her soul, but I, her son, do not know whether I rejoice my mother's soul by what I have done, so I, the young man, say in my soul, my mother is not yet pleased with the property I have given her. That is the meaning of saying I have paid, but have not yet finished paying."

And he said, "Thank you, Ali. And I have understood what you said."

And the sun had begun to shine, and six o'clock had already struck. And the Vizir sat with a joyful spirit. "I am going today to get the Sultanship, for I have known these words and their meaning by my own understanding." And the Vizir waited till nine o'clock, when the Sultan held his audience. And as the Vizir went out of his house, he owned nothing but the one kanzu that was on his body. And he went out with a joyful spirit.

And he went till he arrived before the door of the Sultan. And the people who were there, and all the soldiers who were there, were greatly astonished. "Eh! The great Vizir, who has all the Sultan's affairs in his hands, is coming in a kanzu only, and has not even sandals on his feet." And the people were astonished at him. No one that knew what he had in his soul. And the simple people said, "Perhaps he has lost his wife." And like this he came to the Sultan.

And the Vizir arose and said, "Subalkheir Seyedina."

And the Sultan said, "Allah bilkheir al wazir, come near."

And he sat down.

And the Sultan said, "Tell me your news."

And the Vizir said, "Good news. I have come to give you the meaning of those words, Sultan, about which you and I made mutual promises. And I have known them by my own understanding, Sultan."

And the Sultan said, "Explain to me the first."

And the Vizir said, "When people ask Ali why his property had gone to ruin, he tells them, 'He who does not know the meaning of it, will not be told,' because he would not tell those matters to ignorant people. They would not know how to reply to him. Was it not better, then, not to tell those who knew not its meaning? For he who tells a man a matter, likes to get an answer. Would you tell anything to a man who would not know how to reply? This, then, was his meaning in not telling them."

And the Sultan said, "Yes, certainly, these words are true." And he said, "Give me the meaning, Vizir, of those four parts."

And the Vizir said, "In the first place, Sultan, one part was sunk in the sea, and one part set on fire, and one was lent and he will not be repaid, and one he paid and has not finished his payment."

And the Sultan said, "Yes, Vizir, certainly your words are true." And he said, "Give me the meaning of the one part being sunk in the sea."

And he said, "It is the property with which Ali spent in dissipation and debauchery, and that property was forever lost. That was the meaning of saying that one part had gone into the sea."

And the Sultan said, "Yes, Vizir, certainly that word is true." And the Sultan said, "That money, after it has been sent to women, is not to be had again. His words are true. It is as if it had gone into the sea. Give me also the meaning of the second part, which was set on fire. Give me its meaning."

And the Vizir said, "Ali ate much, and dressed much, and spent much. That is the meaning of setting that property on fire. It returns not again into his hands."

And the Sultan said, "Yes, certainly these words are true, for the property, when you have finished buying food, and you have bought fine clothes, and put them on, the property is lost, and never returns. Ali has spoken his words truly, it is as if it had been set on fire." And he said, "Tell me, Vizir, about the meaning of the third part."

And the Vizir said, "The third part he had lent and will not be repaid."

And the Sultan said, "What is the meaning of lending this property, and he will not be repaid?"

And the Vizir said, "It is the property that he gave to send a dowry to his wife. When you leave her, she does not return your property. This is the meaning of his saying, I have lent and shall not be paid."

And the Sultan said, "Yes, Vizir, certainly these words are true. He that gives a wife a dowry does not get it again. When the husband has gone to ruin, the wife has no good spirit to give to him. Because you have become poor, she looks upon you as a simpleton, she does not know you as having been her husband. Because you have become destitute, you have become bad, too, and more, she looks upon you as a man without understanding, because you have lost your property. For when you had property you were a handsome man, you were a clever youth, you seemed like the son of a Sultan."

And the Vizir arose and said, "True, Sultan, if a man loses his property he is nobody in other people's eyes."

And the Sultan said, "Vizir, tell me the meaning of the fourth part, to pay and not to have finished paying."

And the Vizir said to the Sultan, "Its meaning is that Ali gave the property to his mother. Now Ali knows not whether his mother's soul is satisfied with the property given her by her son. So Ali says, perhaps my mother is not yet pleased with what I have done for her. That is the meaning of Ali's talking of paying and not having finished paying."

The Sultan said, "Yes, Vizir." And he arose from the chair he sat in, and the audience was very full with people, and he called an officer, and said to him, "Go to the fort and order the commander to beat the drums. My Vizir has now become Sultan, and I have become his Vizir, and all you soldiers, and all you who are in the town, Arabs, and Swahili, and Comoro men, obey the Sultan."

And he arose, and the Vizir took the Sultanship. So they remained for the space of two days.

As a man was passing the house which had been the Vizir's, he saw Ali at the window peeping out, and ordering the groom to saddle a horse, for he wanted to ride out. The Arab called to him, "Ali!"

And Ali answered, "Yes."

"Why are you in this house?"

And Ali said, "Did not the Sultan tell me to sell dear, and not cheap, mind you? And I have sold dear."

"What?" The Arab was astonished. "How comes this Ali to be in the house of the great Vizir? Oh well, no matter." And he waited.

Another Arab passed, and saw Ali down in the reception-room, and called to him, "Ali!"

And Ali answered, "Yes."

And the man said, "Why do I find you here, Ali?"

And Ali said, "Is not this my house?"

"How comes this to be your house?"

"The Sultan told me, 'Sell dear, don't sell cheap,' and I have sold dear, mind you."

The Arab arose and went to the old Sultan's door. And he said to him, "My Master, my lord, I have met with your slave Ali, in the house of your old Vizir, and I asked him, 'Ali!' And he answered, 'Yes.' And I said, 'What are you doing in this house?' And Ali answered me, 'The Sultan told me. Sell dear, don't sell cheap, and I have sold dear.'"

The old Sultan was astonished. "This is how the Vizir has served me, and we promised one another to exclude asking Ali. Has he then gone and asked Ali, and is his property gone? Well, now he has lost it twice over. He has lost his old property and now he has lost the Sultanship. And you go quickly and call Ali to come."

"All right, Master."

And he went out running, and found Ali waiting to get into a boat to go on the water. And he called him, "Ali!"

And Ali said, "Yes."

And he said, "Quick!. You are called for at the new Sultan's palace."

And Ali said, "All right, I am like a Sultan, Sultan of myself."

And Ali arose, and went up-stairs and called, "Mrashi, find me something from among the good clothes that are in the chests, for you are the one that knows them best."

And Mrashi went and opened the chest, and she took out a fine joho, and she took out a fine turban, and she took out a shawl for the waist, and she took out a dagger with gold filigree work, and she took out a curved sword of Arab albunsayidi, and she took out a phial of otto of roses of Stamboul, and took them to her Master.

When Ali saw those clothes, he rejoiced, and took and put them on, and went down with the Arab, and they went till they came to the new Sultan's door.

The guards told him, "Pass on into the reception-room." And he passed on and sat down.

When the Sultan came down to hold the audience, there came down also the old Sultan, who was now the Vizir. And the old Sultan, who was now the Vizir said, "Was not our agreement in force? I told you that my agreement was that you should know by your own understanding, without going to ask Ali."

And the new Sultan said, "Yes."

"But you turned round, and went to ask Ali."

But the new Sultan said, "I did not ask Ali."

The old Sultan said, "Ah! Is not this Ali here? Let us call him, so that he may come before us, so that we may believe that you knew these words by your own understanding, without Ali's telling you."

And the new Sultan smiled and said, "Yes, call Ali, let him come."

And the old Sultan arose and called Ali. And he answered, "Here, sir."

And then the old Sultan said, " How is it that you, Ali, should go to live in the Vizir's house? What is your reason?"

And he said, "Yes, Sultan, you told me yourself, 'Sell dear, don't sell cheap,' and this is the note which the Vizir wrote for me. Read it yourself, Sultan, that you may know that these things are true."

The old Sultan took the note and read it, and he said, "True, Ali, you did sell dear, and not cheap."

And the old Sultan arose and called his old Vizir, and he said, "Here, sir." And then he said to the people, "You who are at the audience, great and small, Banyan, and Arab, and Sheheri, and Comoro man, and Swahili, and all the people in the land. Now then, I have taken him away. He has neither the Vizirship nor the Sultanship. His condition is like that of the townspeople. And now this Ali has become my chief Vizir. Everyone, whatever he desires, be it man, or woman, Arab, or European, let all go to Ali. There it is that their business will be concluded."

And this story was made by Ninga.

The One-Handed Girl

This story has been edited and adapted from Andrew Lang's The All Sorts Of Stories Book, first published in 1911 by Longmans, Green and Company of London and New York. Lang's story was taken from the original Swahili Tales by Edward Steere, LL.D.

An old couple once lived in a hut under a grove of palm trees, and they had one son and one daughter. They were all very happy together for many years, and then the father became very ill, and felt he was going to die. He called his children to the place where he lay on the floor - for no one had any beds in that country - and said to his son, "I have no herds of cattle to leave you - only the few things there are in the house - for I am a poor man, as you know. But choose, will you have my blessing or my property?"

"Your property, certainly," answered the son, and his father nodded.

"And you?" asked the old man of the girl, who stood by her brother.

"I will have blessing," she answered, and her father gave her much blessing.

That night he died, and his wife and son and daughter mourned for him seven days, and gave him a burial according to the custom of his people. But hardly was the time of mourning over, than the mother was attacked by a disease which was common in that country.

"I am going away from you," she said to her children, in a faint voice, "but first, my son, choose which you will have, blessing or property."

"Property, certainly," answered the son.

"And you, my daughter?"

"I will have blessing," said the girl, and her mother gave her much blessing, and that night she died.

When the days of mourning were ended, the brother bade his sister put outside the hut all that belonged to his father and his mother. So the girl put them out, and he took them away, save only a small pot and a vessel in which she could clean her corn. But she had no corn to clean.

She sat at home, sad and hungry, when a neighbour knocked at the door.

"My pot has cracked in the fire, lend me yours to cook my supper in, and I will give you a handful of corn in return."

And the girl was glad, and that night she was able to have supper herself, and next day another woman borrowed her pot, and then another and another, for never were known so many accidents as befell the village pots at that time. She soon grew quite fat with all the corn she earned with the help of her pot, and then one evening she picked up a pumpkin seed in a corner, and planted it near her well, and it sprang up, and gave her many pumpkins.

At last it happened that a youth from her village passed through the place where the girl's brother was, and the two met and talked.

"What news is there of my sister?" asked the young man, with whom things had gone badly, for he was idle.

"She is fat and well-liking," replied the youth, "for the women borrow her mortar to clean their corn, and borrow her pot to cook it in, and for all this they give her more food than she can eat." And he went his way.

Now the brother was filled with envy at the words of the man, and he set out at once, and before dawn he had reached the hut, and saw the pot and the mortar were standing outside. He slung them over his shoulders and departed, pleased with his own cleverness, but when his sister awoke and sought for the pot to cook her corn for breakfast, she could find it nowhere.

At length she said to herself, "Well, some thief must have stolen them while I slept. I will go and see if any of my pumpkins are ripe."

And indeed they were, and so many that the tree was almost broken by the weight of them. So she ate what she wanted and took the others to the village, and gave them in exchange for corn, and the women said that no pumpkins were as sweet as these, and that she was to bring every day all that she had. In this way she earned more than she needed for herself, and soon was able to get another mortar and cooking pot in exchange for her corn. Then she thought she was quite rich.

Unluckily someone else thought so too, and this was her brother's wife, who had heard all about the pumpkin tree, and sent her slave with a handful of grain to buy her a pumpkin. At first the girl told him that so few were left that she could not spare any, but when she found that he belonged to her brother, she changed her mind, and went out to the tree and gathered the largest and the ripest that was there.

"Take this one," she said to the slave, "and carry it back to your mistress, but tell her to keep the corn, as the pumpkin is a gift."

The brother's wife was overjoyed at the sight of the fruit, and when she tasted it, she declared it was the nicest she had ever eaten. Indeed, all night she thought of nothing else, and early in the morning she called another slave (for she was a rich woman) and bade him go and ask for another pumpkin. But the girl, who had just been out to look at her tree, told him that they were all eaten, so he went back empty-handed to his mistress.

In the evening her husband returned from hunting a long way off, and found his wife in tears.

"What is the matter?" asked he.

"I sent a slave with some grain to your sister to buy some pumpkins, but she would not sell me any, and told me there were none, though I know she lets other people buy them."

"Well, never mind now - go to sleep," said he, "and tomorrow I will go and pull up the pumpkin tree, and that will punish her for treating you so badly."

So before sunrise he got up and set out for his sister's house, and found her cleaning some corn.

"Why did you refuse to sell my wife a pumpkin yesterday when she wanted one?" he asked.

"The old ones are finished, and the new ones are not yet come," answered the girl. "When her slave arrived two days ago, there were only four left, but I gave him one, and would take no corn for it."

"I do not believe you. You have sold them all to other people. I shall go and cut down the pumpkin," cried her brother in a rage.

"If you cut down the pumpkin you shall cut off my hand with it," exclaimed the girl, running up to her tree and catching hold of it. But her brother followed, and with one blow cut off the pumpkin and her hand too.

Then he went into the house and took away everything he could find, and sold the house to a friend of his who had long wished to have it, and his sister had no home to go to.

Meanwhile she had bathed her arm carefully, and bound on it some healing leaves that grew nearby, and wrapped a cloth round the leaves, and went to hide in the forest, that her brother might not find her again.

For seven days she wandered about, eating only the fruit that hung from the trees above her, and every night she climbed up and tucked herself safely among the creepers which bound together the big branches, so that neither lions nor tigers nor panthers might get at her.

When she woke up on the seventh morning she saw from her perch smoke coming up from a little town on the edge of the forest. The sight of the huts made her feel lonelier and more helpless than before. She longed desperately for a draught of milk from a gourd, for there were no streams in that part, and she was very thirsty, but how was she to earn anything with only one hand? And at this thought her courage failed, and she began to cry bitterly.

It happened that the king's son had come out from the town very early to shoot birds, and when the sun grew hot he felt tired.

"I will lie here and rest under this tree," he said to his attendants. "You can go and shoot instead, and I will just have this slave to stay with me!"

Away they went, and the young man fell asleep, and slept long. Suddenly he was awakened by something wet and salt falling on his face.

"What is that? Is it raining?" he said to his slave. "Go and look."

"No, Master, it is not raining," answered the slave.

"Then climb up the tree and see what it is," and the slave climbed up, and came back and told his Master that a beautiful girl was sitting up there, and that it must have been her tears which had fallen on the face of the king's son.

"Why was she crying?" inquired the prince.

"I cannot tell - I did not dare to ask her, but perhaps she would tell you." And the Master, greatly wondering, climbed up the tree.

"What is the matter with you?" said he gently, and, as she only sobbed louder, he continued, "Are you a woman, or a spirit of the woods?"

"I am a woman," she answered slowly, wiping her eyes with a leaf of the creeper that hung about her.

"Then why do you cry?" he persisted.

"I have many things to cry for," she replied, "more than you could ever guess."

"Come home with me," said the prince, "it is not very far. Come home to my father and mother. I am a king's son."

"Then why are you here?" she said, opening her eyes and staring at him.

"Once every month I and my friends shoot birds in the forest," he answered, "but I was tired and bade them leave me to rest. And you - what are you doing up in this tree?"

At that she began to cry again, and told the king's son all that had befallen her since the death of her mother.

"I cannot come down with you, for I do not like anyone to see me," she ended with a sob.

"Oh! I will manage all that," said the king's son, and swinging himself to a lower branch, he bade his slave go quickly into the town, and bring back with him four strong men and a curtained litter. When the man was gone, the girl climbed down, and hid herself on the ground in some bushes. Very soon the slave returned with the litter, which was placed on the ground close to the bushes where the girl lay.

"Now go, all of you, and call my attendants, for I do not wish to say here any longer," he said to the men, and as soon as they were out of sight he bade the girl get into the litter, and fasten the curtains tightly. Then he got in on the other side, and waited till his attendants came up.

"What is the matter, O son of a king?" asked they, breathless with running.

"I think I am ill. I am cold," he said, and signing to the bearers, he drew the curtains, and was carried through the forest right inside his own house.

"Tell my father and mother that I have a fever, and want some gruel," said he, "and bid them send it quickly."

So the slave hastened to the king's palace and gave his message, which troubled both the king and the queen greatly. A pot of hot gruel was instantly prepared, and carried over to the sick man, and as soon as the council was over, the king and his ministers went to pay him a visit, bearing a message from the queen that she would follow a little later.

Now the prince had pretended to be ill in order to soften his parent's hearts, and the next day he declared he felt better, and, getting into his litter, was carried to the palace in state, drums being beaten all along the road.

He dismounted at the foot of the steps and walked up, a great parasol being held over his head by a slave. Then he entered the cool, dark room where his father and mother were sitting, and said to them, "I saw a girl yesterday in the forest whom I wish to marry, and, unknown to my attendants, I brought her back to my house in a litter. Give me your consent, I beg, for no other woman pleases me as well, even though she has but one hand!"

Of course the king and queen would have preferred a daughter-in-law with two hands, and one who could have brought riches with her, but they could not bear to say "No" to their son, so they told him it should be as he chose, and that the wedding feast should be prepared immediately.

The girl could scarcely believe her good fortune, and, in gratitude for all the kindness shown her, was so useful and pleasant to her husband's parents that they soon loved her.

By and bye a baby was born to her, and soon after that the prince was sent on a journey by his father to visit some of the distant towns of the kingdom, and to set right things that had gone wrong.

No sooner had he started than the girl's brother, who had wasted all the riches his wife had brought him in recklessness and folly, and was now very poor, chanced to come into the town, and as he passed he heard a man say, "Do you know that the king's son has married a woman who has lost one of her hands?" On hearing these words the brother stopped and asked, "Where did he find such a woman?"

"In the forest," answered the man, and the cruel brother guessed at once it must be his sister.

A great rage took possession of his soul as he thought of the girl whom he had tried to ruin being after all so much better off than himself, and he vowed that he would work her ill. Therefore that very afternoon he made his way to the palace and asked to see the king.

When he was admitted to his presence, he knelt down and touched the ground with his forehead, and the king bade him stand up and explain why he had come.

"By the kindness of your heart have you been deceived, O king," said he. "Your son has married a girl who has lost a hand. Do you know why she had lost it? She was a witch, and has wedded three husbands, and each husband she has put to death with her arts. Then the people of the town cut off her hand, and turned her into the forest. And what I say is true, for her town is my town also."

The king listened, and his face grew dark. Unluckily he had a hasty temper, and did not stop to reason, and, instead of sending to the town, and discovering people who knew his daughter-in-law and could have told him how hard she had worked and how poor she had been, he believed all the brother's lying words, and made the queen believe them too. Together they took counsel on what they should do, and in the end they decided that they also would put her out of the town. But this did not content the brother.

"Kill her," he said. "It is no more than she deserves for daring to marry the king's son. Then she can do no more hurt to anyone."

"We cannot kill her," answered they, "if we did, our son would assuredly kill us. Let us do as the others did, and put her out of the town. And with this the envious brother was forced to be content.

The poor girl loved her husband very much, but just then the baby was more to her than all else in the world, and as long as she had him with her, she did not very much mind anything. So, taking her son on her arm, and hanging a little earthen pot for cooking round her neck, she left her house with its great peacock fans and slaves and seats of ivory, and plunged into the forest.

For a while she walked, not knowing where she went. Then by and by she grew tired, and sat under a tree to rest and to hush her baby to sleep. Suddenly she raised her eyes, and saw a snake wriggling from under the bushes towards her.

"I am a dead woman," she said to herself, and stayed quite still, for indeed she was too frightened to move. In another minute the snake had reached her side, and to her surprise he spoke.

"Open your earthen pot, and let me go in. Save me from sun, and I will save you from rain," and she opened the pot, and when the snake had slipped in, she put on the cover. Soon she beheld another snake coming after the other one, and when it had reached her it stopped and said, "Did you see a small grey snake pass this way just now?"

"Yes," she answered, "it was going very quickly."

"Ah, I must hurry and catch it up," replied the second snake, and it hastened on.

When it was out of sight, a voice from the pot said, "Uncover me," and she lifted the lid, and the little grey snake slid rapidly to the ground.

"I am safe now," he said. "But tell me, where are you going?"

"I cannot tell you, for I do not know," she answered. "I am just wandering in the wood."

"Follow me, and let us go home together," said the snake, and the girl followed him through the forest and along the green paths, till they came to a great lake, where they stopped to rest.

"The sun is hot," said the snake, "and you have walked far. Take your baby and bathe in that cool place where the boughs of the tree stretch far over the water."

"Yes, I will," answered she, and they went in. The baby splashed and crowed with delight, and then he gave a spring and fell right in, down, down, down, and his mother could not find him, though she searched all among the reeds.

Full of terror, she made her way back to the bank, and called to the snake, "My baby is gone! He is drowned, and never shall I see him again."

"Go in once more," said the snake, "and feel everywhere, even among the trees that have their roots in the water, lest perhaps he may be held fast there."

Swiftly she went back and felt everywhere with her whole hand, even putting her fingers into the tiniest crannies, where a crab could hardly have taken shelter.

"No, he is not here," she cried. "How am I to live without him?"

But the snake took no notice, and only answered, "Put in your other arm too."

"What is the use of that?" she asked, "when it has no hand to feel with?" but all the same she did as she was bid, and in an instant the wounded arm touched something round and soft, lying between two stones in a clump of reeds.

"My baby, my baby!" she shouted, and lifted him up, merry and laughing, and not a bit hurt or frightened.

"Have you found him this time?" asked the snake.

"Yes, oh, yes!" she answered, "and, why - why - I have got my hand back again!" and from sheer joy she burst into tears.

The snake let her weep for a little while, and then he said, "Now we will journey on to my family, and we will all repay you for the kindness you showed to me."

"You have done more than enough in giving me back my hand," replied the girl, but the snake only smiled.

"Be quick, lest the sun should set," he answered, and began to wriggle along so fast that the girl could hardly follow him.

By and by they arrived at the house in a tree where the snake lived, when he was not travelling with his father and mother. And he told them all his adventures, and how he had escaped from his enemy. The father and mother snake could not do enough to show their gratitude. They made their guest lie down on a hammock woven of the strong creepers which hung from bough to bough, till she was quite rested after her wanderings, while they watched the baby and gave him milk to drink from the cocoa-nuts which they persuaded their friends the monkeys to crack for them. They even managed to carry small fruit tied up in their tails for the baby's mother, who felt at last that she was safe and at peace. Not that she forgot her husband, for she often thought of him and longed to show him her son, and in the night she would sometimes lie awake and wonder where he was.

In this manner many weeks passed by. And what was the prince doing?

Well, he had fallen very ill when he was on the furthest border of the kingdom, and he was nursed by some kind people who did not know who he was, so that the king and queen heard nothing about him. When he was better he made his way home again, and into his father's palace, where he found a strange man standing behind the throne with the peacock's feathers. This was his wife's brother, whom the king had taken into high favour, though, of course, the prince was quite ignorant of what had happened.

For a moment the king and queen stared at their son, as if he had been unknown to them, for he had grown so thin and weak during his illness that his shoulders were bowed like those of an old man.

"Have you forgotten me so soon?" he asked.

At the sound of his voice they gave a cry and ran towards him, and poured out questions as to what had happened, and why he looked like that. But the prince did not answer any of them.

"How is my wife?" he said. There was a pause.

Then the queen replied, "She is dead."

"Dead!" he repeated, stepping a little backwards. "And my child?"

"He is dead too."

The young man stood silent. Then he said, "Show me their graves."

At these words the king, who had been feeling rather uncomfortable, took heart again, for had he not prepared two beautiful tombs for his son to see, so that he might never, never guess what had been done to his wife? All these months the king and queen had been telling each other how good and merciful they had been not to take her brother's advice and to put her to death. But now, this somehow did not seem so certain.

Then the king led the way to the courtyard just behind the palace, and through the gate into a beautiful garden where stood two splendid tombs in a green space under the trees. The prince advanced alone, and, resting his head against the stone, he burst into tears. His father and mother stood silently behind with a curious pang in their souls which they did not quite understand. Could it be that they were ashamed of themselves?

But after a while the prince turned round, and walking past them into the palace, he bade the slaves bring him mourning. For seven days no one saw him, but at the end of them he went out hunting, and helped his father rule his people. Only no one dared to speak to him of his wife and son.

At last one morning, after the girl had been lying awake all night thinking of her husband, she said to her friend the snake, "You have all shown me much kindness, but now I am well again, and want to go home and hear some news of my husband, and if he still mourns for me!"

Now the heart of the snake was sad at her words, but he only said, "Yes, thus it must be. Go and bid farewell to my father and mother, but if they offer you a present, see that you take nothing but my father's ring and my mother's casket."

So she went to the parent snakes, who wept bitterly at the thought of losing her, and offered her gold and jewels as much as she could carry in remembrance of them. But the girl shook her head and pushed the shining heap away from her.

"I shall never forget you, never," she said in a broken voice, "but the only tokens I will accept from you are that little ring and this old casket."

The two snakes looked at each other in dismay. The ring and the casket were the only things they did not want her to have. Then after a short pause they spoke. "Why do you want the ring and casket so much? Who has told you of them?"

"Oh, nobody. It is just my fancy," answered she. But the old snakes shook their heads and replied, "Not so. It is our son who told you, and, as he said, so it must be. If you need food, or clothes, or a house, tell the ring and it will find them for you. And if you are unhappy or in danger, tell the casket and it will set things right." Then they both gave her their blessing, and she picked up her baby and went her way.

She walked for a long time, till at length she came near the town where her husband and his father dwelt. Here she stopped under a grove of palm trees, and told the ring that she wanted a house.

"It is ready, mistress," whispered a queer little voice which made her jump, and, looking behind her, she saw a lovely palace made of the finest woods, and a row of slaves with tall fans bowing before the door. Glad indeed was she to enter, for she was very tired, and, after eating a good supper of fruit and milk which she found in one of the rooms, she flung herself down on a pile of cushions and went to sleep with her baby beside her.

Here she stayed quietly, and every day the baby grew taller and stronger, and very soon he could run about and even talk. Of course the neighbours had a great deal to say about the house which had been built so quickly - so very quickly - on the outskirts of the town, and invented all kinds of stories about the rich lady who lived in it. And by and by, when the king returned with his son from the wars, some of these tales reached his ears.

"It is really very odd about that house under the palms," he said to the queen, "I must find out something about the lady whom no one ever sees. I daresay it is not a lady at all, but a gang of conspirators who want to get possession of my throne. Tomorrow I shall take my son and my chief ministers and insist on getting inside."

Soon after sunrise next day the prince's wife was standing on a little hill behind the house, when she saw a cloud of dust coming through the town. A moment afterwards she heard faintly the roll of the drums that announced the king's presence, and saw a crowd of people approaching the grove of palms. Her heart beat fast. Could her husband be among them? In any case they must not discover her there, so just bidding the ring prepare some food for them, she ran inside, and bound a veil of golden gauze round her head and face. Then, taking the child's hand, she went to the door and waited.

In a few minutes the whole procession came up, and she stepped forward and begged them to come in and rest.

"Willingly," answered the king, "go first, and we will follow you."

They followed her into a long dark room, in which was a table covered with gold cups and baskets filled with dates and cocoa-nuts and all kinds of ripe yellow fruits, and the king and the prince sat upon cushions and were served by slaves, while the ministers, among whom she recognised her own brother, stood behind.

"Ah, I owe all my misery to him," she said to herself. "From the first he has hated me," but outwardly she showed nothing. And when the king asked her what news there was in the town she only answered, "You have ridden far. Eat first, and drink, for you must be hungry and thirsty, and then I will tell you my news."

"You speak sense," answered the king, and silence prevailed for some time longer. Then he said, "Now, lady, I have finished, and am refreshed, therefore tell me, I pray you, who you are, and from where you come? But, first, be seated."

She bowed her head and sat down on a big scarlet cushion, drawing her little boy, who was asleep in a corner, on to her knee, and began to tell the story of her life. As her brother listened, he would fain have left the house and hidden himself in the forest, but it was his duty to wave the fan of peacock's feathers over the king's head to keep off the flies, and he knew he would be seized by the royal guards if he tried to desert his post. He must stay where he was, there was no help for it, and luckily for him the king was too much interested in the tale to notice that the fan had ceased moving, and that flies were dancing right on the top of his head.

The story went on, but the story-teller never once looked at the prince, even through her veil, though he on his side never moved his eyes from her. When she reached the part where she had sat weeping in the tree, the king's son could restrain himself no longer.

"It is my wife," he cried, springing to where she sat with the sleeping child in her lap. "They have lied to me, and you are not dead after all, nor the boy either! But what has happened? Why did they lie to me? And why did you leave my house where you were safe?" And he turned and looked fiercely at his father.

"Let me finish my tale first, and then you will know," answered she, throwing back her veil, and she told how her brother had come to the palace and accused her of being a witch, and had tried to persuade the king to slay her. "But he would not do that," she continued softly, "and after all, if I had stayed on in your house, I should never have met the snake, nor have got my hand back again. So let us forget all about it, and be happy once more, for see! Our son is growing up to be quite a big boy."

"And what shall be done to your brother?" asked the king, who was glad to think that someone had acted in this matter worse than himself.

"Put him out of the town, without a hand!" answered she.

The Kites And The Crows

This story has been edited and adapted from George W. Bateman's Zanzibar Tales, Told by Natives of the East Coast of Africa, first published in 1901 by A. C. McClurg and Company in Chicago. The original stories were translated from the original Swahili and illustrated by Walter Bobbett.

One day Koongooroo, Sultan of the crows, sent a letter to Mwayway, Sultan of the kites, containing these few words, "I want you folks to be my soldiers."

To this brief message Mwayway at once wrote this short reply, "I should say not."

Thereupon, thinking to scare Mwayway, the Sultan of the crows sent him word, "If you refuse to obey me I'll make war upon you."

To which the Sultan of the kites replied, "That suits me. Let us fight, and if you beat us we will obey you, but if we are victors you shall be our servants."

So they gathered their forces and engaged in a great battle, and in a little while it became evident that the crows were being badly beaten.

As it appeared certain that, if something were not done pretty quickly, they would all be killed, one old crow, named Jeeoosee, suddenly proposed that they should fly away.

Directly the suggestion was made it was acted upon, and the crows left their homes and flew far away, where they set up another town. So, when the kites entered the place, they found no one there, and they took up their residence in Crowtown.

One day, when the crows had gathered in council, Koongooroo stood up and said, "My people, do as I command you, and all will be well. Pluck out some of my feathers and throw me into the town of the kites, then come back and stay here until you hear from me."

Without argument or questioning the crows obeyed their Sultan's command.

Koongooroo had lain in the street but a short time, when some passing kites saw him and inquired threateningly, "What are you doing here in our town?"

With many a moan he replied, "My companions have beaten me and turned me out of their town because I advised them to obey Mwayway, Sultan of the kites."

When they heard this they picked him up and took him before the Sultan, to whom they said, "We found this fellow lying in the street, and he attributes his involuntary presence in our town to so singular a circumstance that we thought you should hear his story."

Koongooroo was then bidden to repeat his statement, which he did, adding the remark that, much as he had suffered, he still held to his opinion that Mwayway was his rightful Sultan.

This, of course, made a very favourable impression, and the Sultan said, "You have more sense than all the rest of your tribe put together, I guess you can stay here and live with us."

So Koongooroo, expressing much gratitude, settled down, apparently, to spend the remainder of his life with the kites.

One day his neighbours took him to church with them, and when they returned home they asked him, "Who has the best kind of religion, the kites or the crows?"

To which crafty old Koongooroo replied, with great enthusiasm, "Oh, the kites, by long odds!"

This answer tickled the kites like anything, and Koongooroo was looked upon as a bird of remarkable discernment.

When almost another week had passed, the Sultan of the crows slipped away in the night, went to his own town, and called his people together.

"Tomorrow," said he, "is the great annual religious festival of the kites, and they will all go to church in the morning. Go, now, and get some wood and some fire, and wait near their town until I call you. Then come quickly and set fire to the church."

Then he hurried back to Mwayway's town.

The crows were very busy indeed all that night, and by dawn they had an abundance of wood and fire at hand, and were lying in wait near the town of their victorious enemies.

So in the morning every kite went to church. There was not one person left at home except old Koongooroo.

When his neighbours called for him they found him lying down. "Why!" they exclaimed with surprise, "are you not going to church today?"

"Oh," said he, "I wish I could, but my stomach aches so badly I can't move!" And he groaned dreadfully.

"Ah, poor fellow!" said they, "you will be better in bed," and they left him to himself.

As soon as everybody was out of sight he flew swiftly to his soldiers and cried, "Come on, they're all in the church."

Then they all crept quickly but quietly to the church, and while some piled wood about the door, others applied fire.

The wood caught readily, and the fire was burning fiercely before the kites were aware of their danger, but when the church began to fill with smoke, and tongues of flame shot through the cracks, they tried to escape through the windows. The greater part of them, however, were suffocated, or, having their wings singed, could not fly away, and so were burned to death, and among the corpses was the charred body of their Sultan, Mwayway. Koongooroo and his crows had got their old town back again.

And that is why, from that day to this, the kites fly away from the crows.

Thunder And The Gods

This story is based on a traditional Maasai folk tale, of which there are many variations. This adaptation is my own simple version based on my reading of a number of those sources.

Once upon a time there were two gods. One was a black god and the other was a red god. The black god was very humble, kind and loving, while the red god was malevolent and did not care about people at all. These gods lived together way up in heaven, but the black god wanted to live closer to people, so he lived underneath the red god.

One day famine spread across the world. Cattle could not find any grass to eat nor water to drink. They were dying from starvation. Then the black god spoke to the red god and said, "Let us give people water for they are about to starve to death."

The red god was at first reluctant because he really did not like people, but after much pleading from the black god, he relented. The gods agreed that they should let the rains fall from heaven to earth, and when this was done, it rained very hard for many days.

A while later, the red god said, "You can stop the rains now, for the people have enough."

The black god answered, "No, let's leave it for a few more days, for the earth has been parched dry like a desert."

They let the rains fall for a few more days, and when this was done, the red god again told the black god to hold back the water. He did that and so the rain stopped falling.

A few more days went by and the black god once more asked the red god to let the rains fall for the people. This time the red god refused, which led to a huge argument. The red god threatened to wipe out all of the people. He thought they had been spoiled and deserved nothing less. The black god had a real struggle but did manage to prevent the red god from killing everyone.

And so, even today, when you hear loud thunder, it is the red god who is trying to get past the black god to wipe out all of the people on earth. So far, the black god has always prevailed.

An Indian Tale

This story has been edited and adapted from Edward Steere's Swahili Tales, originally published in 1870 by Bell and Daldy, York Street, Covent Garden, London.

There was once an Indian Sultan who had one son, and he loved him very much. And when he was dying, he said to his Vizirs, "Give the kingdom to my son, and love him very much, even as I have done." Then he died.

And they ended their mourning, and the lad governed. And the Vizir had a son of his own, and those youths were very fond of one another, and they went on spending their money and wealth in many ways and for many days, until they had spent the kingdom too.

One day the Sultan's son said to the Vizir's son, "Let us travel and see various towns." And they got ready a ship, and put in it provisions, and money, and soldiers, and set out on their journey.

While at sea they were wrecked, and many of the people died. The Vizir's son was eaten by a shark, and one of his slaves was carried away by the water. The Sultan's son and one of his slaves were saved, and washed up near a strange city in Africa.

When they reached the town, they stopped in the fields, and the Sultan's son said to his slave, "Go into the town and look for food, and let us come and eat."

When the slave arrived in the town there were games going on, and many people were crowded together. The Sultan of the town had died, and they were looking for another Sultan to put in his place. They used to throw a lime, and whoever it struck three times then became the new Sultan.

The line was thrown the first time, and it struck that slave lad. And they looked at him and said, "It is of no use, throw a second time." And they threw, and it struck that slave lad. And they made him go away from where he was, and set him in a place at some considerable distance. And they threw the line out again for the third time, and still it struck the slave lad. And they said, "So then it is he who is to be our Sultan."

And the Vizirs took the slave lad, and went with him through the city, with rejoicing and games, and many cannons were fired. And they made him rule over the kingdom, and he enjoyed this immensely.

In that city there was a Bedouin, who slaughtered animals and sold goats' flesh. And he used to slaughter people, and mix their flesh with his meat. This was his employment, and those who were in the town knew nothing of it.

The Sultan's son came into the town and passed by the Bedouin's door. The Bedouin he took hold of him, and pulled him inside, and fastened him in the stocks. And there were many people bound along with the goats. Now in the morning, one person and a goat were taken and killed, and their flesh was mixed together, and the Bedouin then went and sold it from the seat at his door. And every day this was what he did. The Sultan's son was very thin through grief, so he called one of the Bedouin's slaves and gave him a small coin. And he gave it to him and said, "Buy me some thread and a little bit of cloth." And the slave bought it, and brought it to him. And he stitched a beautiful cap, and wrote verses inside the cap. He wrote:

Ajabtu rangadida na kitun hiraja Illahi

Eke kordenai, eke kordeshire,

Raja bondekana, gulam batashahi;

Ajabtu rangadida, kitun hiraja Illahi.

He gave it to the Bedouin, who was very glad of it, and he said to the Bedouin, "Go and sell this cap at the new Sultan's house. It is there where you will get its price."

And the Bedouin went and sold it. When the Sultan saw it, he knew that the work of that cap was his Master's. And he read the verses, too, and knew their meaning, and their meaning was this:

"A Wonder from God,

One was taken by the water,

One was taken by the shark,

I, a free man, am bound,

My slave has got a kingdom,

The new Sultan asked the Bedouin, "Where did you get this cap?"

And he said, "It was my wife who made it."

And the Sultan gave him fifty dollars, and said, "Tell your wife to make me another."

And the Bedouin went on his way.

Then the new Sultan, the former slave, chose soldiers, and told them, "Follow after him, and when you see the house he goes into, return and come and tell me."

And they followed the Bedouin home. And he went inside. The soldiers returned and told the Sultan, and said, "We have seen his house."

One hundred soldiers were chosen to go to the house with orders to, "Seize him and bind him, and bring all the people that are in his house, that you may come to the palace with them."

The soldiers went and seized the Bedouin, and bound him, and came with him, and with all the people that were in his house. And he was asked, "Is this your employment, to seize people and bind them in your house, to kill them, and give them to people to eat?"

And he could not deny it.

And the people were asked, and they said, "This is what he does."

And he was imprisoned in the fort.

And then the new Sultan took his Master and ordered some people to give him a bath, and give him clothes, and he dressed. He took food, and he ate and was satisfied. And then he asked his old slave what had happened. He told him all. "And I am sultan here in the town, but to-morrow I will resign it and give it to you, my Master. I dare not be sultan before you."

In the morning all of the people in the town gathered, and they went to the Sultan, who adorned his Master bravely, and clothed him with the royal robes. And when the pair came out, their dress and roles reversed, the people wondered - what sort of news is this?

And the slave Sultan said, " Have you given me this kingship in truth, or in jest?"

And the Vizirs said, "We have given it you in truth."

And so he asked, "What pleases me, does it please you also?"

And they answered, "It pleases us."

And he said, "It pleases me that this man should be our Sultan."

And they answered, "We consent." Then they asked, "Who is this man?"

Their former Sultan said, "This is my rightful Master and Sultan there at home, but this is God's ordering."

And those that were in the town had great joy. And that Bedouin was drowned, and all his property was given to the poor. And they lived in peace and enjoyment till the end.

The Ape, The Snake, And The Lion

This story has been edited and adapted from George W. Bateman's Zanzibar Tales, Told by Natives of the East Coast of Africa, first published in 1901 by A. C. McClurg and Company in Chicago. The original stories were translated from the original Swahili and illustrated by Walter Bobbett.

Long, long ago there lived, in a village called Keejeejee, a woman whose husband died, leaving her with a little baby boy. She worked hard all day to get food for herself and child, but they lived very poorly and were most of the time half-starved.

When the boy, whose name was Mvoo Laana, began to get big, he said to his mother, one day, "Mother, we are always hungry. What work did my father do to support us?"

His mother replied, "Your father was a hunter. He set traps, and we ate what he caught in them."

"Oho!" said Mvoo Laana, "That's not work, that's fun. I, too, will set traps, and see if we can't get enough to eat."

The next day he went into the forest and cut branches from the trees, and returned home in the evening.

The second day he spent making the branches into traps.

The third day he twisted cocoanut fiber into ropes.

The fourth day he set up as many traps as time would permit.

The fifth day he set up the remainder of the traps.

The sixth day he went to examine the traps, and they had caught so much game, beside what they needed for themselves, that he took a great quantity to the big town of Oongooja, where he sold it and bought corn and other things, and the house was full of food, and, as this good fortune continued, he and his mother lived very comfortably.

But after a while, when he went to his traps he found nothing in them day after day.

One morning, however, he found that an ape had been caught in one of the traps, and he was about to kill it, when it said, "Son of Adam, I am Neeanee, the ape. Do not kill me. Take me out of this trap and let me go. Save me from the rain, that I may come and save you from the sun someday."

So Mvoo Laana took him out of the trap and let him go.

When Neeanee had climbed up in a tree, he sat on a branch and said to the youth, "For your kindness I will give you a piece of advice. Believe me, men are all bad. Never do a good turn for a man. If you do, he will do you harm at the first opportunity."

The next day, Mvoo Laana found a snake in the same trap. He started to the village to give the alarm, but the snake shouted, "Come back, son of Adam. Don't call the people from the village to come and kill me. I am Neeoka, the snake. Let me out of this trap, I pray you. Save me from the rain today, that I may be able to save you from the sun tomorrow, if you should be in need of help."

So the youth let him go, and as he went he said, "I will return your kindness if I can, but do not trust any man. If you do him a kindness he will do you an injury in return at the first opportunity."

The third day, Mvoo Laana found a lion in the same trap that had caught the ape and the snake, and he was afraid to go near it. But the lion said, "Don't run away. I am Simba Kongway, the very old lion. Let me out of this trap, and I will not hurt you. Save me from the rain, that I may save you from the sun if you should need help."

So Mvoo Laana believed him and let him out of the trap, and Simba Kongway, before going his way, said, "Son of Adam, you have been kind to me, and I will repay you with kindness if I can, but never do a kindness to a man, or he will pay you back with unkindness."

The next day a man was caught in the same trap, and when the youth released him, he repeatedly assured him that he would never forget the service he had done him in restoring his liberty and saving his life.

Well, it seemed that he had caught all the game that could be taken in traps, and Mvoo Laana and his mother were hungry every day, with nothing to satisfy them, just as they had been before. At last he said to his mother, one day, "Mother, make me seven cakes of the little meal we have left, and I will go hunting with my bow and arrows." So she baked him the cakes, and he took them and his bow and arrows and went into the forest.

The youth walked and walked, but could see no game, and finally he found that he had lost his way, and had eaten all his cakes but one.

And he went on and on, not knowing whether he was going away from his home or toward it, until he came to the wildest and most desolate looking wood he had ever seen. He was so wretched and tired that he felt he must lie down and die, when suddenly he heard someone calling him, and looking up he saw Neeanee, the ape, who said, "Son of Adam, where are you going?"

"I don't know," replied Mvoo Laana, sadly, "I'm lost."

"Well, well," said the ape, "don't worry. Just sit down here and rest yourself until I come back, and I will repay with kindness the kindness you once showed me."

Then Neeanee went away off to some gardens and stole a whole lot of ripe paw-paws and bananas, and brought them to Mvoo Laana, and said, "Here's plenty of food for you. Is there anything else you want? Would you like a drink?" And before the youth could answer he ran off with a calabash and brought it back full of water. So the youth ate heartily, and drank all the water he needed, and then each said to the other, "Good-bye, till we meet again," and went their separate ways.

When Mvoo Laana had walked a great deal farther without finding which way he should go, he met Simba Kongway, who asked, "Where are you going, son of Adam?"

And the youth answered, as dolefully as before, "I don't know. I'm lost."

"Come, cheer up," said the very old lion, "and rest yourself here a little. I want to repay with kindness today the kindness you showed me on a former day."

So Mvoo Laana sat down. Simba Kongway went away, but soon returned with some game he had caught, and then he brought some fire, and the young man cooked the game and ate it. When he had finished he felt a great deal better, and they bade each other good-bye for the present, and each went his way.

After he had travelled another very long distance the youth came to a farm, and was met by a very, very old woman, who said to him, "Stranger, my husband has been taken very sick, and I am looking for someone to make him some medicine. Won't you make it?"

But he answered, "My good woman, I am not a doctor, I am a hunter, and never used medicine in my life. I cannot help you."

When he came to the road leading to the principal city he saw a well, with a bucket standing near it, and he said to himself, "That's just what I want. I'll take a drink of nice well-water. Let me see if the water can be reached."

As he peeped over the edge of the well, to see if the water was high enough, what should he behold but a great big snake, which, directly it saw him, said, "Son of Adam, wait a moment." Then it came out of the well and said, "How? Don't you know me?"

"I certainly do not," said the youth, stepping back a little.

"Well, well!" said the snake, "I could never forget you. I am Neeoka, whom you released from the trap. You know I said, 'Save me from the rain, and I will save you from the sun.' Now, you are a stranger in the town to which you are going. Therefore hand me your little bag, and I will place in it the things that will be of use to you when you arrive there."

So Mvoo Laana gave Neeoka the little bag, and he filled it with chains of gold and silver, and told him to use them freely for his own benefit. Then they parted very cordially.

When the youth reached the city, the first man he met was he whom he had released from the trap, who invited him to go home with him, which he did, and the man's wife made him supper.

As soon as he could get away unobserved, the man went to the Sultan and said, "There is a stranger come to my house with a bag full of chains of silver and gold, which he says he got from a snake that lives in a well. But although he pretends to be a man, I know that he is a snake who has power to look like a man."

When the Sultan heard this he sent some soldiers who brought Mvoo Laana and his little bag before him. When they opened the little bag, the man who was released from the trap persuaded the people that some evil would come out of it, and affect the children of the Sultan and the children of the Vizir.

Then the people became excited, and tied the hands of Mvoo Laana behind him.

But the great snake had come out of the well and arrived at the town just about this time, and he went and lay at the feet of the man who had said all those bad things about Mvoo Laana, and when the people saw this they said to that man, "How is this? There is the great snake that lives in the well, and he stays by you. Tell him to go away."

But Neeoka would not stir. So they untied the young man's hands, and tried in every way to make amends for having suspected him of being a wizard.

Then the Sultan asked him, "Why should this man invite you to his home and then speak ill of you?"

And Mvoo Laana related all that had happened to him, and how the ape, the snake, and the lion had cautioned him about the results of doing any kindness for a man.

And the Sultan said, "Although men are often ungrateful, they are not always so. Only the bad ones. As for this fellow, he deserves to be put in a sack and drowned in the sea. He was treated kindly, and returned evil for good."

The Warrior Who Went To God's Country

This story is based on a traditional Maasai folk tale, of which there are many variations. This adaptation is my own simple version based on my reading of a number of those sources.

Many years ago a raiding party of young warriors set off on a cattle raid, and while travelling, one of the warrior's sandals broke and he had to sit down to repair it. As he did so, he said to the others, "My friends, please wait for me."

His companions said, "Not us. Ask whoever is coming up last to wait with you."

The young warrior asked a second group of warriors the same question and they replied with the same answer.

When the last warrior eventually came by, the young man said, "Please wait for me, friend."

This last warrior said, "I will place a branch on the path that we take when I get to the fork on the path, then you can follow that path and catch up with us." So saying he hurried to catch up with the others.

The young man with the broken sandal saw the wisdom in this and continued to mend his sandal.

The last warrior went on, and when he got to the next fork in the path he cut a branch and placed it on the path to show direction that the other warriors had taken. Sadly, as the warriors went on, a strong wind came and blew the branch onto another path entirely. When the warrior with the broken sandal got to the spot after repairing his sandal, he found the branch and he followed it quickly so that he might catch up with his friends.

As he went along, he spotted the moon, which was grazing quietly, and he stopped to stare at the moon. The moon asked him, "You there, young warrior, where have you come from and where are you going?"

The warrior answered, "I am far from home and we are off on a cattle raid, but the other warriors left me behind when my sandal broke. I stopped to repair it."

The moon then asked, "When you look at me, what do you think I look like?"

"Oh, you look very fine to me," answered the warrior.

The moon thought for a moment and said, "You may go on and when you come across anybody, do not tell them what they look like, just tell them they look fine. Do not take anything along the way, and when you are given a choice between a good and bad thing choose the bad thing."

With this advice ringing in his ears, the young warrior continued on his journey.

Soon he came upon a river with flowing water. As he was about to cross it, the river said to him, "You there, young warrior, have a drink before you cross me."

The warrior answered, "Let me cross you first, and then I will take a drink from the far bank." He crossed the river, but then he went on without drinking any water.

Soon after that he came upon a river of milk, and as he was about to step into it, this milky river also asked him to take a drink before crossing over to the far bank. The warrior, however, did exactly as he had before and crossed without taking a drink of milk.

Finally he came upon a river of blood, and once again, the same thing happened. He crossed all the three rivers without drinking from any of them.

As the warrior continued on his journey, he came upon two swords that were sharpening themselves. They said to the warrior, "You there, young warrior, sharpen us. Then you can take the best blade for your own. "

The warrior said, "Let me walk on a little way, then I will come back and sharpen you." He went past the swords and then just continued with his journey.

Next he walked up to delicious looking pieces of meat that were frying on their own. The meat said to him, "You there, young warrior, stir us and eat the juiciest one of us."

The warrior again managed to trick the meat as he had done with the three rivers and with the swords.

A little while later, the warrior found two axes that were fighting each other. They stopped for a moment and said, "You there, young warrior, please separate us and stop our fighting. If you do that you can take one of us to your mother to hew wood with."

The warrior simply said, "Hold on a little while, I'll be right back."

He went on with his journey as he had done at every stage before. Whenever he now came upon something new, he played the same trick with it, and left without doing anything or picking anything up. He left everything behind.

Eventually, he came up to a man who was herding God's cattle. This man had two heads, and all the cattle had two tails. After exchanging greetings the cattle-herd asked the warrior, "What do I look like? How do you find me?"

"Oh, you look just like everybody else," answered the warrior.

"And how do you find these cows?" the old man asked.

The warrior replied, "They are like all other cattle."

The old man then gave the young warrior some new directions, and they parted company.

The warrior carried on walking, and every time that he thought he was about to reach God's house, the house seemed to move away from him, but he walked on with much patience, and eventually he reached God's house. There was a lady there, a lady of God, who asked the young warrior, "Would you like fresh or stale milk to drink?"

The warrior answered, "What use do I have for fresh milk when stale milk is in plenty!" He was given fresh milk.

Later on, just before bedtime, the old lady again asked the warrior, "Would you want curdled or fresh milk?"

The warrior said he wanted fresh milk, but he was given curdled milk to drink.

Time passed and soon it was the time for sleep. The old lady asked the warrior whether he wanted a bed that had been cleared of dust or one that was covered with dust. The warrior chose the bed covered with dust, and was, instead, showed to a clean and soft bed, and he was soon soundly asleep.

As the dawn sun rose into the sky, the old lady woke the warrior up and said, "I want you to stay inside and when you hear the sound of thunder you must not utter a sound or come outside."

The warrior did as he was instructed. In a few minutes he heard the sound of thunder and the house vibrated. The warrior remained inside the house, sitting quiet and still, until the old lady invited him outside. When he went outside he found a large herd of cattle together with sheep, goats and donkeys.

The lady said to him, "All this is yours. Drive it and go in peace."

The warrior took the cattle and returned to his country. As he was nearing his village some clouds of dust could be seen a short distance away. It turned out that after waiting for a long time for their companion with the broken sandal, the other warriors had finally given up on their friend, assuming that he had been eaten by wild beasts. He was mourned by his family. But then the warrior arrived with his enormous herd of cattle, goats, sheep and donkeys.

When the people and his families asked him how he had obtained the cattle, he told them the whole story about his journey into God's country.

So, when fortunate warrior's brother heard his story, he made up his mind to go to God's country as well, so that he might come back with a huge herd. His fortunate brother forbade him to go, saying, "Please do not go, for you are not able to do the things I did."

But his brother insisted, saying, "I must go, brother."

The warrior's brother went on and on until he came upon the moon. The moon talked to him in the same way he had talked to his brother, and asked him, "What do you think of me?"

"I have never ever seen anything like you!" answered the warrior in astonishment

The moon gave him directions, and he proceeded on the same path as his brother.

On coming upon the river of water, the river asked him to have a drink before crossing. He knelt down and drank to his fill before crossing. He also drank from the river of milk and from the river of blood, crossing them all after doing so.

Then he came upon swords that were sharpening themselves, and when the swords asked him to sharpen them and take the sharpest, he did so, leaving with the sharpest. Likewise, he found meat that was frying itself. He sat down, cooked it and ate the cooked bits. When he found the fighting axes, he separated them, and took one along as they had asked him to. He did everything that his brother had not done.

He next came upon the two-headed man as he was grazing two-tailed cattle. They talked together for a little while, and the old man posed the same question he had put to his brother, "How do you find me?"

The warrior boldly answered, "You have two heads."

"And how do you find these cattle?" continued the old man.

"They each have two tails," added the warrior.

The old man, nonetheless, directed the warrior to God's village and returned to tend his cattle.

He walked on. When God's house moved as he was about to enter it, he hit it with his club and it stopped. When the old lady asked him to choose between fresh and stale milk he said, "Why should I choose stale milk when there is fresh milk!" He was given stale milk.

At bedtime, he said he did not want fresh milk, he wanted curdled milk. He was given fresh milk.

He chose a fine clean bed and he was given one with ashes.

He was given all the bad things when he expressed preference for good ones.

Very early the next morning, the old lady told him to remain still and not to utter a sound nor leave the house when he heard the sound of thunder. But no sooner had he heard the sound of thunder than he shot up and went outside to check on what was making the sound. The lady once more asked him to go back to the house. But once again, as soon as he heard the sound of thunder, he rushed outside.

He did this over and over again, and eventually the lady said to him, "You must go, you do not deserve property."

He returned to his country empty handed, but for the axe, the sword and the other weapons.

The end.

The Cheat And The Porter

This story has been edited and adapted from Edward Steere's Swahili Tales, originally published in 1870 by Bell and Daldy, York Street, Covent Garden, London.

There was a man, who was a cheat, who used to go and buy things, and when he had bought them he did not give any money to the men who had to carry his goods.

One day he bought a box of glasses, and he looked for a man to carry them for him. He found a porter and said to him, "Choose your price for your hire, or I will say three words to you that will be of service to you in the wider world."

The porter thought about this and said, "I get money every day. I will carry your glasses for those three words that you shall tell me."

And he carried the box. And when he had got a third of the way, he said, "Master, this box is heavy. It is too much for me. Give me one word, that I may get spirit to go on."

And the cheat said, "If anyone tells you that slavery is better than freedom, don't believe him."

And the porter looked hard at the man, and knew instantly what was what. He muttered to himself, "The owner of this box is a cheat, but I had better wait till I get to the end."

And so they went on, and when they had gone another third of the way, the porter said, "Tell me the second word."

And the man said, "If anyone tells you that poverty is better than riches, don't believe him."

And they went on. When they reached the man's house the porter said, "Master, tell me the third word."

The man said, "Put it down."

The porter said, "I am exceedingly pleased with the two words you have told me. Tell me the third, that I may get to set it down in my memory."

And the man said, "If anyone tells you that hunger is better than fulness, don't believe him."

And the porter said, "Move out of the way, Master, so that I may set this heavy box down." And then he lifted the box of glasses above his head and let it fall to the ground.

The owner said, "Ah! Ah! You have broken my box for me!"

And the porter replied, "If anyone tells you that there is one glass left in this box that is not broken, don't believe him."

Haamdaanee

This story has been edited and adapted from George W. Bateman's Zanzibar Tales, Told by Natives of the East Coast of Africa, first published in 1901 by A. C. McClurg and Company in Chicago. The original stories were translated from the original Swahili and illustrated by Walter Bobbett.

Once there was a very poor man, named Haamdaanee, who begged from door to door for his living, sometimes taking things before they were offered him. After a while people became suspicious of him, and stopped giving him anything, in order to keep him away from their houses. So at last he was reduced to the necessity of going every morning to the village dust heap, and picking up and eating the few grains of the tiny little millet seed that he might find there.

One day, as he was scratching and turning over the heap, he found a dime, which he tied up in a corner of his ragged dress, and continued to hunt for millet grains, but could not find one.

"Oh, well," said he, "I've got a dime now, so I'm pretty well fixed. I'll go home and take a nap instead of a meal."

So he went to his hut, took a drink of water, put some tobacco in his mouth, and went to sleep.

The next morning, as he scratched in the dust heap, he saw a countryman going along, carrying a basket made of twigs, and he called to him, "Hi, there, countryman! What have you in that cage?"

The countryman, whose name was Moohaadeem, replied, "Gazelles."

And Haamdaanee called, "Bring them here. Let me see them."

Now there were three well-to-do men standing near, and when they saw the countryman coming to Haamdaanee they smiled, and said, "You're taking lots of trouble for nothing, Moohaadeem."

"How's that, gentlemen?" he inquired.

"Why," said they, "that poor fellow has nothing at all. Not a cent."

"Oh, I don't know that," said the countryman, "he may have plenty, for all I know."

"Not he," said they.

"Don't you see for yourself," continued one of them, "that he is on the dust heap? Every day he scratches there like a hen, trying to get enough grains of millet to keep himself alive. If he had any money, wouldn't he buy a square meal, for once in his life? Do you think he would want to buy a gazelle? What would he do with it? He can't find enough food for himself, without looking for any for a gazelle."

But Moohaadeem said, "Gentlemen, I have brought some goods here to sell. I answer all who call me, and if anyone says 'Come,' I go to him. I don't favour one and slight another;. As this man called me, I'm going to him."

"All right," said the first man, "you don't believe us. Well, we know where he lives, and all about him, and we know that he can't buy anything."

"That's so," said the second man. "Perhaps, however, you will see that we were right, after you have a talk with him."

To which the third man added, "Clouds are a sign of rain, but we have seen no signs of his being about to spend any money."

"All right, gentlemen," said Moohaadeem, "many better-looking people than he call me, and when I show them my gazelles they say, 'Oh, yes, they're very beautiful, but awfully dear. Take them away.' So I shall not be disappointed if this man says the same thing. I shall go to him, anyhow."

Then one of the three men said, "Let us go with this man, and see what the beggar will buy."

"Pshaw!" said another, "Buy! You talk foolishly. He has not had a good meal in three years, to my knowledge, and a man in his condition doesn't have money to buy gazelles. However, let's go, and if he makes this poor countryman carry his load over there just for the fun of looking at the gazelles, let each of us give him a good hard whack with our walking-sticks, to teach him how to behave toward honest merchants."

So, when they came near him, one of those three men said, "Well, here are the gazelles, so now buy one. Here they are, you old hypocrite. You'll feast your eyes on them, but you can't buy them."

But Haamdaanee, paying no attention to the men, said to Moohaadeem, "How much for one of your gazelles?"

Then another of those men broke in, "You're very innocent, aren't you? You know, as well as I do, that gazelles are sold every day at two for a quarter."

Still taking no notice of these outsiders, Haamdaanee continued, "I'd like to buy one for a dime."

"One for a dime!" laughed the men, "Of course you'd like to buy one for a dime. Perhaps you'd also like to have the dime to buy with."

Then one of them gave him a push on the cheek.

At this Haamdaanee turned and said, "Why do you push me on the cheek, when I've done nothing to you? I do not know you. I call this man, to transact some business with him, and you, who are strangers, step in to spoil our trade."

He then untied the knot in the corner of his ragged coat, produced the dime, and, handing it to Moohaadeem, said, "Please, good man, let me have a gazelle for that."

At this, the countryman took a small gazelle out of the cage and handed it to him, saying, "Here, Master, take this one. I call it Keejeepaa."

Then turning to those three men, he laughed, and said, "Ehe! How's this? You, with your white robes, and turbans, and swords, and daggers, and sandals on your feet - you gentlemen of property, and no mistake - you told me this man was too poor to buy anything, yet he has bought a gazelle for a dime, while you fine fellows, I think, haven't enough money among you to buy half a gazelle, if they were five cents each."

Then Moohaadeem and the three men went their several ways.

As for Haamdaanee, he stayed at the dust heap until he found a few grains of millet for himself and a few for Keejeepaa, the gazelle, and then went to his hut, spread his sleeping mat, and he and the gazelle slept together.

This going to the dust heap for a few grains of millet and then going home to bed continued for about a week.

Then one night Haamdaanee was awakened by someone calling, "Master!" Sitting up, he answered, "Here I am. Who calls?"

The gazelle answered, "I do!"

Upon this, the beggar man became so scared that he did not know whether he should faint or get up and run away.

Seeing him so overcome, Keejeepaa asked, "Why, Master, what's the matter?"

"Oh, gracious!" he gasped, "what a wonder I see!"

"A wonder?" said the gazelle, looking all around, "Why, what is this wonder, that makes you act as if you were all broken up?"

"Why, it's so wonderful, I can hardly believe I'm awake!" said his Master. "Who in the world ever before knew of a gazelle that could speak?"

"Oho!" laughed Keejeepaa, "Is that all? There are many more wonderful things than that. But now, listen, while I tell you why I called you."

"Certainly. I'll listen to every word," said the man. "I can't help listening!"

"Well, you see, it's just this way," said Keejeepaa, "I've allowed you to become my Master, and I cannot run away from you, so I want you to make an agreement with me, and I will make you a promise, and keep it."

"Say on," said his Master.

"Now," continued the gazelle, "one doesn't have to be acquainted with you long, in order to discover that you are very poor. This scratching a few grains of millet from the dust heap every day, and managing to subsist upon them, is all very well for you - you're used to it, because it's a matter of necessity with you, but if I keep it up much longer, you won't have any gazelle - Keejeepaa will die of starvation. Therefore, I want to go away every day and feed on my own kind of food, and I promise you I will return every evening."

"Well, I guess I'll have to give my consent," said the man, in no very cheerful tone.

As it was now dawn, Keejeepaa jumped up and ran out of the door, Haamdaanee following him. The gazelle ran very fast, and his Master stood watching him until he disappeared. Then tears started in the man's eyes, and, raising his hands, he cried, "Oh, my mother!" Then he cried, "Oh, my father!" Then he cried, "Oh, my gazelle! It has run away!"

Some of his neighbours, who heard him carrying on in this manner, took the opportunity to inform him that he was a fool, an idiot, and a dissipated fellow.

Said one of them, "You hung around that dust heap, goodness knows how long, scratching like a hen, till fortune gave you a dime. You hadn't sense enough to go and buy some decent food. You had to buy a gazelle. Now you've let the creature run away. What are you crying about? You brought all your trouble on yourself."

All this, of course, was not very comforting to Haamdaanee, who slunk off to the dust heap, got a few grains of millet, and came back to his hut, which now seemed meaner and more desolate than ever.

At sunset, however, Keejeepaa came trotting in, and the beggar was happy again, and said, "Ah, my friend, you have returned to me."

"Of course," said the gazelle, "didn't I promise you? You see, I feel that when you bought me you gave all the money you had in the world, even though it was only a dime. Why, then, should I grieve you? I couldn't do it. If I go and get myself some food, I'll always come back evenings."

When the neighbours saw the gazelle come home every evening and run off every morning, they were greatly surprised, and began to suspect that Haamdaanee was a wizard.

Well, this coming and going continued for five days, the gazelle telling its Master each night what fine places it had been to, and what lots of food it had eaten.

On the sixth day it was feeding among some thorn bushes in a thick wood, when, scratching away some bitter grass at the foot of a big tree, it saw an immense diamond of intense brightness.

"Oho!" said Keejeepaa, in great astonishment, "here's property, and no mistake! This is worth a kingdom! If I take it to my Master he will be killed, for, being a poor man, if they say to him, 'Where did you get it?' and he answers, 'I picked it up,' they will not believe him. If he says, 'It was given to me,' they will not believe him either. It will not do for me to get my Master into difficulties. I know what I'll do. I'll seek some powerful person, who will use it properly."

So Keejeepaa started off through the forest, holding the diamond in his mouth, and ran, and ran, but saw no town that day, so he slept in the forest, and arose at dawn and pursued his way. And the second day passed like the first.

On the third day the gazelle had travelled from dawn until between eight and nine o'clock, when he began to see scattered houses, getting larger in size, and knew he was approaching a town. In due time he found himself in the main street of a large city, leading directly to the Sultan's palace, and began to run as fast as he could. People passing along stopped to look at the strange sight of a gazelle running swiftly along the main street with something wrapped in green leaves between its teeth.

The Sultan was sitting at the door of his palace, when Keejeepaa, stopping a little way off, dropped the diamond from its mouth, and, lying down beside it, panting, called out, "Ho, there! Ho, there!" which is a cry everyone makes in that part of the world when wishing to enter a house, remaining outside until the cry is answered.

After the cry had been repeated several times, the Sultan said to his attendants, "Who is doing all that calling?"

And one answered, "Master, it's a gazelle that's calling, 'Ho, there!'"

"Ho-ho!" said the Sultan, "Ho-ho! Invite the gazelle to come near."

Then three attendants ran to Keejeepaa and said, "Come, get up. The Sultan commands you to come near."

So the gazelle arose, picked up the diamond, and, approaching the Sultan, laid the jewel at his feet, saying, "Master, good afternoon!"

The Sultan replied, "May God make it good! Come near."

The Sultan ordered his attendants to bring a carpet and a large cushion, and desired the gazelle to rest upon them. When it protested that it was comfortable as it was, he insisted, and Keejeepaa had to allow himself to be made a very honoured guest. Then they brought milk and rice, and the Sultan would hear nothing until the gazelle had fed and rested.

At last, when everything had been disposed of, the Sultan said, "Well, now, my friend, tell me what news you bring."

And Keejeepaa said, "Master, I don't exactly know how you will like the news I bring. The fact is, I'm sent here to insult you! I've come to try and pick a quarrel with you! In fact, I'm here to propose a family alliance with you!"

At this the Sultan exclaimed, "Oh, come! For a gazelle, you certainly know how to talk! Now, the fact of it is, I'm looking for someone to insult me. I'm just aching to have someone pick a quarrel with me. I'm impatient for a family alliance. Go on with your message."

Then Keejeepaa said, "You don't bear any ill will against me, who am only a messenger?"

And the Sultan said, "None at all."

"Well," said Keejeepaa, "look at this pledge I bring," dropping the diamond wrapped in leaves into the Sultan's lap.

When the Sultan opened the leaves and saw the great, sparkling jewel, he was overcome with astonishment. At last he said, "Well?"

"I have brought this pledge," said the gazelle, "from my Master, Sultan Daaraaee. He has heard that you have a daughter, so he sent you this jewel, hoping you will forgive him for not sending something more worthy of your acceptance than this trifle."

"Goodness!" said the Sultan to himself, "he calls this a trifle!" Then to the gazelle, "Oh, that's all right, that's all right. I'm satisfied. The Sultan Daaraaee has my consent to marry my daughter, and I don't want a single thing from him. Let him come empty-handed. If he has more of these trifles, let him leave them at home. This is my message, and I hope you will make it perfectly clear to your Master."

The gazelle assured him that he would explain everything satisfactorily, adding, "And now, Master, I take my leave. I go straight to our own town, and hope that in about eleven days we shall return to be your guests." So, with mutual compliments, they parted.

In the meantime, Haamdaanee was having an exceedingly tough time. Keejeepaa having disappeared, he wandered about the town moaning, "Oh, my poor gazelle! My poor gazelle!" while the neighbours laughed and jeered at him, until, between them and his loss, he was nearly out of his mind.

But one evening, when he had gone to bed, Keejeepaa walked in. Up he jumped, and began to embrace the gazelle, and weep over it, and carry on at a great rate.

When he thought there had been about enough of this kind of thing, the gazelle said, "Come, come, keep quiet, my Master. I've brought you good news." But the beggar man continued to cry and fondle, and declare that he had thought his gazelle was dead.

At last Keejeepaa said, "Oh, well, Master, you see I'm all right. You must brace up, and prepare to hear my news, and do as I advise you."

"Go on, go on," replied his Master, "explain what you will, I'll do whatever you require me to do. If you were to say, 'Lie down on your back, that I may roll you over the side of the hill,' I would lie down."

"Well," said the gazelle, "there is not much to explain just now, but I'll tell you this. I've seen many kinds of food, food that is desirable and food that is objectionable, but this food I'm about to offer you is very sweet indeed."

"What?" said Haamdaanee. "Is it possible that in this world there is anything that is positively good? There must be good and bad in everything. Food that is both sweet and bitter is good food, but if food were nothing but sweetness would it not be injurious?"

"H'm!" yawned the gazelle, "I'm too tired to talk philosophy. Let's go to sleep now, and when I call you in the morning, all you have to do is to get up and follow me."

So at dawn they set forth, the gazelle leading the way, and for five days they journeyed through the forest.

On the fifth day they came to a stream, and Keejeepaa said to his Master, "Lie down here." When he had done so, the gazelle set to and beat him so soundly that he cried out, "Oh, let up, I beg of you!"

"Now," said the gazelle, "I'm going away, and when I return I expect to find you right here, so don't you leave this spot on any account." Then he ran away, and about ten o'clock that morning he arrived at the house of the Sultan.

Now, ever since the day Keejeepaa left the town, soldiers had been placed along the road to watch for and announce the approach of Sultan Daaraaee, so one of them, when he saw the gazelle in the distance, rushed up and cried to the Sultan, "Sultan Daaraaee is coming! I've seen the gazelle running as fast as it can in this direction."

The Sultan and his attendants immediately set out to meet his guests, but when they had gone a little way beyond the town they met the gazelle coming along alone, who, on reaching the Sultan, said, "Good day, my Master." The Sultan replied in kind, and asked the news, but Keejeepaa said, "Ah, do not ask me. I can scarcely walk, and my news is bad!"

"Why, how is that?" asked the Sultan.

"Oh, dear!" sighed the gazelle, "Such misfortune and misery! You see, Sultan Daaraaee and I started alone to come here, and we got along all right until we came to the thick part of the forest yonder, when we were met by robbers, who seized my Master, bound him, beat him, and took everything he had, even stripping off every stitch of his clothing. Oh, dear! oh, dear!"

"Dear me!" said the Sultan, "we must attend to this at once."

So, hurrying back with his attendants to his house, he called a groom, to whom he said, "Saddle the best horse in my stable, and put on him my finest harness."

Then he directed a woman servant to open the big inlaid chest and bring him a bag of clothes. When she brought it he picked out a loin-cloth, and a long white robe, and a black over-jacket, and a shawl for the waist, and a turban cloth, all of the very finest. Then he sent for a curved sword with a gold hilt, and a curved dagger with gold filigree, and a pair of elegant sandals, and a fine walking-cane.

Then the Sultan said to Keejeepaa, "Take some of my soldiers, and let them convey these things to Sultan Daaraaee, that he may dress himself and come to me."

But the gazelle answered, "Ah, my Master, can I take these soldiers with me and put Sultan Daaraaee to shame? There he lies, beaten and robbed, and I would not have anyone see him. I can take everything by myself."

"Why," exclaimed the Sultan, "here is a horse, and there are clothes and arms. I don't see how a little gazelle can manage all those things."

But the gazelle had them fasten everything on the horse's back, and tie the end of the bridle around his own neck, and then he set off alone, amidst the wonder and admiration of the people of that city, high and low.

When he arrived at the place where he had left the beggar-man, he found him lying waiting for him, and overjoyed at his return.

"Now," said he, "I have brought you the sweet food I promised. Come, get up and bathe yourself."

With the hesitation of a person long unaccustomed to such a thing, the man stepped into the stream and began to wet himself a little.

"Oh," said the gazelle, impatiently, "a little water like that won't do you much good. Get out into the deep pool."

"Dear me!" said the man, timidly, "There is so much water there, and where there is much water there are sure to be horrible animals."

"Animals! What kind of animals?"

"Well, crocodiles, water lizards, snakes, and, at any rate, frogs, and they bite people, and I'm terribly afraid of all of them."

"Oh, well," said Keejeepaa, "do the best you can in the stream, but rub yourself well with earth, and, for goodness' sake, scrub your teeth well with sand, for they are awfully dirty."

So the man obeyed, and soon made quite a change in his appearance.

Then the gazelle said, "Here, hurry up and put on these things. The sun has gone down, and we ought to have started before this."

So the man dressed himself in the fine clothes the Sultan had sent, and then he mounted the horse, and they started, the gazelle trotting on ahead.

When they had gone some distance, the gazelle stopped, and said, "See here. Nobody who sees you now would suspect that you are the man who scratched in the dust heap yesterday. Even if we were to go back to our town the neighbours would not recognize you, if it were only for the fact that your face is clean and your teeth are white. Your appearance is all right, but I have a caution to give you. Over there, where we are going, I have procured for you the Sultan's daughter for a wife, with all the usual wedding gifts. Now, you must keep quiet. Say nothing except, 'How d'ye do?' and 'What's the news?' Let me do the talking."

"All right," said the man, "that suits me exactly."

"Do you know what your name is?"

"Of course I do."

"Indeed? Well, what is it?"

"Why, my name is Haamdaanee."

"Not much," laughed Keejeepaa, "your name is Sultan Daaraaee."

"Oh, is it?" said his Master. "That's good."

So they started forward again, and in a little while they saw soldiers running in every direction, and fourteen of these joined them to escort them. Then they saw ahead of them the Sultan, and the Vizirs, and the emirs, and the judges, and the great men of the city, coming to meet them.

"Now, then," said Keejeepaa, "get off your horse and salute your father-in-law. That's him in the middle, wearing the sky-blue jacket."

"All right," said the man, jumping off his horse, which was then led by a soldier.

So the two met, and the Sultans shook hands, and kissed each other, and walked up to the palace together.

Then they had a great feast, and made merry and talked until night, at which time Sultan Daaraaee and the gazelle were put into an inner room, with three soldiers at the door to guard and attend upon them.

When the morning came, Keejeepaa went to the Sultan and said, "Master, we wish to attend to the business which brought us here. We want to marry your daughter, and the sooner the ceremony takes place, the better it will please the Sultan Daaraaee."

"Why, that's all right," said the Sultan, "the bride is ready. Let someone call the teacher, Mwaaleemoo, and tell him to come at once."

When Mwaaleemoo arrived, the Sultan said, "See here, we want you to marry this gentleman to my daughter right away."

"All right, I'm ready," said the teacher. So they were married.

Early the next morning the gazelle said to his Master, "Now I'm off on a journey. I shall be gone about a week, but however long I am gone, don't you leave the house till I return. Good-bye."

Then he went to the real Sultan and said, "Good Master, Sultan Daaraaee has ordered me to return to our town and put his house in order. He commands me to be here again in a week. If I do not return by that time, he will stay here until I come."

The Sultan asked him if he would not like to have some soldiers go with him, but the gazelle replied that he was quite competent to take care of himself, as his previous journeys had proved, and he preferred to go alone, so with mutual good wishes they parted.

But Keejeepaa did not go in the direction of the old village. He struck off by another road through the forest, and after a time came to a very fine town, of large, handsome houses. As he went through the principal street, right to the far end, he was greatly astonished to observe that the town seemed to have no inhabitants, for he saw neither man, woman, nor child in all the place.

At the end of the main street he came upon the largest and most beautiful house he had ever seen, built of sapphire, and turquoise, and costly marbles.

"Oh, my!" said the gazelle, "This house would just suit my Master. I'll have to pluck up my courage and see whether this is deserted like the other houses in this mysterious town."

So Keejeepaa knocked at the door, and called, "Hello, there!" several times, but no one answered. And he said to himself, "This is strange! If there were no one inside, the door would be fastened on the outside. Perhaps they are in another part of the house, or asleep. I'll call again, louder."

So he called again, very loud and long, "Hel-lo, th-e-re! Hel-lo!" And directly an old woman inside answered, "Who is that calling so loudly?"

"It is I, your grandchild, good mistress," said Keejeepaa.

"If you are my grandchild," replied the old woman, "go back to your home at once and don't come and die here, and bring me to my death also."

"Oh, come," said he, "open the door, mistress, I have just a few words I wish to say to you."

"My dear grandson," she replied, "the only reason why I do not open the door is because I fear to endanger both your life and my own."

"Oh, don't worry about that. I guess your life and mine are safe enough for a while. Open the door, anyhow, and hear the little I have to say."

So the old woman opened the door.

Then they exchanged salutations and compliments, after which she asked the gazelle, "What's the news from your place, grandson?"

"Oh, everything is going along pretty well," said he, "what's the news around here?"

"Ah!" sighed the old creature, "The news here is very bad. If you're looking for a place to die in, you've struck it here. I've not the slightest doubt you'll see all you want of death this very day."

"Huh!" replied Keejeepaa, lightly, "For a fly to die in honey is not bad for the fly, and doesn't injure the honey."

"It may be all very well for you to be easy about it," persisted the old person, "but if people with swords and shields did not escape, how can a little thing like you avoid danger? I must again beg of you to go back to the place you came from. Your safety seems of more interest to me than it is to you."

"Well, you see, I can't go back just now, and besides, I want to find out more about this place. Who owns it?"

"Ah, grandson, in this house are enormous wealth, numbers of people, hundreds of horses, and the owner is Neeoka Mkoo, the wonderfully big snake. He owns this whole town, also."

"Oho! Is that so?" said Keejeepaa. "Look here, old lady, can't you put me on to some plan of getting near this big snake, that I may kill him?"

"Mercy!" cried the old woman, in affright, "don't talk like that. You've put my life in danger already, for I'm sure Neeoka Mkoo can hear what is said in this house, wherever he is. You see I'm a poor old woman, and I have been placed here, with those pots and pans, to cook for him. Well, when the big snake is coming, the wind begins to blow and the dust flies as it would do in a great storm. Then, when he arrives in the courtyard, he eats until he is full, and after that, goes inside there to drink water. When he has finished, he goes away again. This occurs every other day, just when the sun is overhead. I may add that Neeoka Mkoo has seven heads. Now, then, do you think yourself a match for him?"

"Look here, mother," said the gazelle, "don't you worry about me. Has this big snake a sword?"

"He has. This is it," said she, taking from its peg a very keen and beautiful blade, and handing it to him, "but what's the use in bothering about it? We are dead already."

"We shall see about that," said Keejeepaa.

Just at that moment the wind began to blow, and the dust to fly, as if a great storm were approaching.

"Do you hear the great one coming?" cried the old woman.

"Pshaw!" said the gazelle, "I'm a great one also - and I have the advantage of being on the inside. Two bulls can't live in one cattle-pen. Either he will live in this house, or I will."

Notwithstanding the terror the old lady was in, she had to smile at the assurance of this little undersized gazelle, and repeated over again her account of the people with swords and shields who had been killed by the big snake.

"Ah, stop your gabbling!" said the gazelle, "You can't always judge a banana by its colour or size. Wait and see, grandma."

In a very little while the big snake, Neeoka Mkoo, came into the courtyard, and went around to all the pots and ate their contents. Then he came to the door.

"Hello, old lady," said he, "how is it I smell a new kind of odour inside there?"

"Oh, that's nothing, good Master," replied the old woman, "I've been so busy around here lately I haven't had time to look after myself, but this morning I used some perfume, and that's what you smell."

Now, Keejeepaa had drawn the sword, and was standing just inside the doorway, so, when the big snake put his head in, it was cut off so quickly that its owner did not know it was gone. When he put in his second head it was cut off with the same quickness, and, feeling a little irritation, he exclaimed, "Who's inside there, scratching me?" He then thrust in his third head, and that was cut off also.

This continued until six heads had been disposed of, when Neeoka Mkoo unfolded his rings and lashed around so that the gazelle and the old woman could not see one another through the dust.

Then the snake thrust in his seventh head, and the gazelle, crying, "Now your time has come. You've climbed many trees, but this you cannot climb," severed it, and immediately fell down in a fainting fit.

Well, that old woman, although she was seventy-five years of age, jumped, and shouted, and laughed, like a girl of nine. Then she ran and got water, and sprinkled the gazelle, and turned him this way and that way, until at last he sneezed, which greatly pleased the old person, who fanned him and tended him until he was quite recovered.

"Oh, my!" said she, "Who would have thought you could be a match for him, my grandson?"

"Well, well," said Keejeepaa, "that's all over. Now show me everything around this place."

So she showed him everything, from top to bottom, store-rooms full of goods, chambers full of expensive foods, rooms containing handsome people who had been kept prisoners for a long time, slaves, and everything.

Next he asked her if there was any person who was likely to lay claim to the place or make any trouble, and she answered, "No one. Everything here belongs to you."

"Very well, then," said he, "you stay here and take care of these things until I bring my Master. This place belongs to him now."

Keejeepaa stayed three days examining the house, and said to himself, "Well, when my Master comes here he will be much pleased with what I have done for him, and he'll appreciate it after the life he's been accustomed to. As to his father-in-law, there is not a house in his town that can compare with this."

On the fourth day he departed, and in due time arrived at the town where the Sultan and his Master lived. Then there were great rejoicings. The Sultan was particularly pleased at his return, while his Master felt as if he had received a new lease of life.

After everything had settled down a little, Keejeepaa told his Master he must be ready to go, with his wife, to his new home after four days. Then he went and told the Sultan that Sultan Daaraaee desired to take his wife to his own town in four days, to which the Sultan strongly objected, but the gazelle said it was his Master's wish, and at last everything was arranged.

On the day of the departure a great company assembled to escort Sultan Daaraaee and his bride. There were the bride's ladies-in-waiting, and slaves, and horsemen, and Keejeepaa leading them all.

So they travelled three days, resting when the sun was overhead, and stopping each evening about five o'clock to eat and sleep, arising next morning at day-break, eating, and going forward again. And all this time the gazelle took very little rest, going all through the company, from the ladies to the slaves, and seeing that everyone was well supplied with food and quite comfortable. Because of this the entire company loved him and valued him like the apples of their eyes.

On the fourth day, during the afternoon, many houses came into view, and some of the folks called Keejeepaa's attention to them. "Certainly," said he, "that is our town, and that house you see yonder is the palace of Sultan Daaraaee."

So they went on, and all the company filed into the courtyard, while the gazelle and his Master went into the house.

When the old woman saw Keejeepaa, she began to dance, and shout, and carry on, just as she did when he killed Neeoka Mkoo, and taking up his foot she kissed it, but Keejeepaa said, "Old lady, let me alone. The one to be made much of is this my Master, Sultan Daaraaee. Kiss his feet. He has the first honours whenever he is present."

The old woman excused herself for not knowing the Master, and then Sultan Daaraaee and the gazelle went around on a tour of inspection. The Sultan ordered all the prisoners to be released, the horses to be sent out to pasture, all the rooms to be swept, the furniture to be dusted, and, in the meantime, servants were busy preparing food. Then everyone had apartments assigned to them, and all were satisfied.

After they had remained there some time, the ladies who had accompanied the bride expressed a desire to return to their own homes. Keejeepaa begged them not to hurry away, but after a while they departed, each loaded with gifts by the gazelle, for whom they had a thousand times more affection than for his Master. Then things settled down to their regular routine.

One day the gazelle said to the old woman, "I think the conduct of my Master is very singular. I have done nothing but good for him all the time I have been with him. I came to this town and braved many dangers for him, and when all was over I gave everything to him. Yet he has never asked, 'How did you get this house? How did you get this town? Who is the owner of this house? Have you rented all these things, or have they been given you? What has become of the inhabitants of the place?' I don't understand him. And further, although I have done nothing but good for him, he has never done one good thing for me. Nothing here is really his. He never saw such a house or town as this since the day he was born, and he doesn't own anything of it. I believe the old folks were right when they said, 'If you want to do any person good, don't do too much. Do him a little harm occasionally, and he'll think more of you.' However, I've done all I can now, and I'd like to see him make some little return."

Next morning the old woman was awakened early by the gazelle calling, "Mother! Mother!" When she went to him she found he was sick in his stomach, feverish, and all his legs ached.

"Go," said he, "and tell my Master I am very ill."

So she went upstairs and found the Master and mistress sitting on a marble couch, covered with a striped silk scarf from India.

"Well," said the Master, "what do you want, old woman?"

"Oh, my Master," cried she, "Keejeepaa is sick!"

The mistress started and said, "Dear me! What is the matter with him?"

"All his body pains him. He is sick all over."

"Oh, well," said the Master, "what can I do? Go and get some of that red millet, that is too common for our use, and make him some gruel."

"Gracious!" exclaimed his wife, staring at him in amazement, "Do you wish her to feed our friend with stuff that a horse would not eat if he were ever so hungry? This is not right of you."

"Ah, get out!" said he, "You're crazy. We eat rice. Isn't red millet good enough for a gazelle that cost only a dime?"

"Oh, but he is no ordinary gazelle. He should be as dear to you as the apple of your eye. If sand got in your eye it would trouble you."

"You talk too much," returned her husband. Then, turning to the old woman, he said, "Go and do as I told you."

So the old woman went downstairs, and when she saw the gazelle, she began to cry, and say, "Oh, dear! Oh, dear!"

It was a long while before the gazelle could persuade her to tell him what had passed upstairs, but at last she told him all. When he had heard it, he said, "Did he really tell you to make me red millet gruel?"

"Ah," cried she, "do you think I would say such a thing if it were not so?"

"Well," said Keejeepaa, "I believe what the old folks said was right. However, we'll give him another chance. Go up to him again, and tell him I am very sick, and that I can't eat that gruel."

So she went upstairs, and found the Master and mistress sitting by the window, drinking coffee.

The Master, looking around and seeing her, said, "What's the matter now, old woman?"

And she said, "Master, I am sent by Keejeepaa. He is very sick indeed, and has not taken the gruel you told me to make for him."

"Oh, bother!" he exclaimed. "Hold your tongue, and keep your feet still, and shut your eyes, and stop your ears with wax. Then, if that gazelle tells you to come up here, say that your legs are stiff. If he tells you to listen, say your ears are deaf, and if he tells you to look, say your sight has failed you. If he wants you to talk, tell him your tongue is paralyzed."

When the old woman heard these words, she stood and stared, and was unable to move. As for his wife, her face became sad, and the tears began to start from her eyes, observing which, her husband said, sharply, "What's the matter with you, Sultan's daughter?"

The lady replied, "A man's madness is his undoing."

"Why do you say that, mistress?" he inquired.

"Ah," said she, "I am grieved, my husband, at your treatment of Keejeepaa. Whenever I say a good word for the gazelle you dislike to hear it. I pity you that your understanding is gone."

"What do you mean by talking in that manner to me?" he blustered.

"Why, advice is a blessing, if properly taken. A husband should advise with his wife, and a wife with her husband. Then they are both blessed."

"Oh, stop," said her husband, impatiently, "it's evident you've lost your senses. You should be chained up."

Then he said to the old woman, "Never mind her talk, and as to this gazelle, tell him to stop bothering me and putting on style, as if he were the Sultan. I can't eat, I can't drink, I can't sleep, because of that gazelle worrying me with his messages. First, the gazelle is sick, then, the gazelle doesn't like what he gets to eat. Confound it! If he likes to eat, let him eat. If he doesn't like to eat, let him die and be out of the way. My mother is dead, and my father is dead, and I still live and eat. Shall I be put out of my way by a gazelle, that I bought for a dime, telling me he wants this thing or that thing? Go and tell him to learn how to behave himself toward his superiors."

When the old woman went downstairs, she found the gazelle was bleeding at the mouth, and in a very bad way. All she could say was, "My son, the good you did is all lost, but be patient."

And the gazelle wept with the old woman when she told him all that had passed, and he said, "Mother, I am dying, not only from sickness, but from shame and anger at this man's ingratitude."

After a while Keejeepaa told the old woman to go and tell the Master that he believed he was dying. When she went upstairs she found Daaraaee chewing sugar-cane, and she said to him, "Master, the gazelle is worse. We think him nearer to dying than getting well."

To which he answered, "Haven't I told you often enough not to bother me?"

Then his wife said, "Oh, husband, won't you go down and see the poor gazelle? If you don't like to go, let me go and see him. He never gets a single good thing from you."

But he turned to the old woman and said, "Go and tell that nuisance of a gazelle to die eleven times if he chooses to."

"Now, husband," persisted the lady, "what has Keejeepaa done to you? Has he done you any wrong? Such words as yours people use to their enemies only. Surely the gazelle is not your enemy. All the people who know him, great and lowly, love him dearly, and they will think it very wrong of you if you neglect him. Now, do be kind to him, Sultan Daaraaee."

But he only repeated his assertion that she had lost her wits, and would have nothing further of argument.

So the old woman went down and found the gazelle worse than ever.

In the meantime Sultan Daaraaee's wife managed to give some rice to a servant to cook for the gazelle, and also sent him a soft shawl to cover him and a pillow to lie upon. She also sent him a message that if he wished, she would have her father's best physicians attend him.

All this was too late, however, for just as these good things arrived, Keejeepaa died.

When the people heard he was dead, they went running around crying and having an awful time, and when Sultan Daaraaee found out what all the commotion was about he was very indignant, remarking, "Why, you are making as much fuss as if I were dead, and all over a gazelle that I bought for a dime!"

But his wife said, "Husband, it was this gazelle that came to ask me of my father, it was he who brought me from my father's, and it was to him I was given by my father. He gave you everything good, and you do not possess a thing that he did not procure for you. He did everything he could to help you, and you not only returned him unkindness, but now he is dead you have ordered people to throw him into the well. Let us alone, that we may weep."

But the gazelle was taken and thrown into the well.

Then the lady wrote a letter telling her father to come to her directly, and despatched it by trusty messengers, upon the receipt of which the Sultan and his attendants started hurriedly to visit his daughter.

When they arrived, and heard that the gazelle was dead and had been thrown into the well, they wept very much, and the Sultan, and the Vizir, and the judges, and the rich chief men, all went down into the well and brought up the body of Keejeepaa, and took it away with them and buried it.

Now, that night the lady dreamt that she was at home at her father's house, and when dawn came she awoke and found she was in her own bed in her own town again.

And her husband dreamed that he was on the dust heap, scratching, and when he awoke there he was, with both hands full of dust, looking for grains of millet. Staring wildly he looked around to the right and left, saying, "Oh, who has played this trick on me? How did I get back here, I wonder?"

Just then the children going along, and seeing him, laughed and hooted at him, calling out, "Hello, Haamdaanee, where have you been? Where do you come from? We thought you were dead long ago."

So the Sultan's daughter lived in happiness with her people until the end, and that beggar-man continued to scratch for grains of millet in the dust heap until he died.

If this story is good, the goodness belongs to all. If it is bad, the badness belongs only to him who told it.

Story Of Liongo

This story has been edited and adapted from Edward Steere's Swahili Tales, originally published in 1870 by Bell and Daldy, York Street, Covent Garden, London.

In the times when Shanga was a flourishing city, there was a man whose name was Liongo, and he had great strength, and was a very great man in the city. And he oppressed the people exceedingly, till one day they made a plan to go to him to his house and bind him. And a great number of people went and came upon him suddenly into his house, and seized him and bound him, and went with him to the prison, and put him into it.

And he stayed many days, and made a plot to get loose. And he went outside the town and harassed the people in the same way for many days. People could not go into the country, neither to cut wood nor to draw water. And they were in much trouble.

And the people said, "What stratagem can we resort to, to get him and kill him?"

And one said, "Let us go against him while he is sleeping, and kill him out of the way."

Others said, "If you get him, bind him and bring him." And they went and made a stratagem so as to take him, and they bound him, and took him to the town. And they went and bound him with chains and fetters and a post between his legs.

And they left him many days, and his mother used to send him food every day. And before the door where he was bound soldiers were set, who watched him. They never went away except by turns.

Many days and many months had passed. Every day, night by night, he used to sing beautiful songs, and everyone who heard them used to be delighted with those songs. Everyone used to say to his friend, "Let us go and listen to Liongo's songs, which he sings in his room." And they used to go and listen. Every day when night came people used to go and say to him, "We have come to sing your songs, let us hear them." And he used to sing, he could not refuse, and the people in the town were delighted with them. And every day he composed different ones, through his grief at being bound. The people knew those songs little by little, but he and his mother and her slave knew them well. And his mother knew the meaning of those songs, and the people in the town did not.

At last one day their slave girl had brought some food, and the soldiers took it from her and ate it, and some scraps were left, and those they gave her. The slave girl told her Master, "I brought food, and these soldiers have taken it from me and eaten it. There remain these scraps."

And he said to her, "Give me them." And he received them and ate, and thanked God for what he had got.

And he said to the slave girl (and he was inside and the slave girl outside the door), "You, slave girl, shall be sent to tell my mother I am a simpleton. I have not yet learnt the ways of the world. Let her make a cake, in the middle be put files, that I may cut my fetters, and the chains may be opened, that I may enter the road, that I may glide like a snake, that I may mount the roofs and walls, that I may look this way and that." And then he said, "Greet my mother well, tell her what I have told you."

And she went and told his mother, and said, "Your son greets you well, he has told me a message to come and tell you."

And his mother said, "What message?"

And she told her what she had been told.

And his mother understood it, and went away to a shop and bought grain, which she gave to her slave to clean. And she went and bought many files. And she took the flour, and made many fine cakes. And. she took the bran and made a large cake, and took the files and, put them into it, and gave them all to her slave to take to him.

And the slave girl went with them, and arrived at the door, and the soldiers robbed her, and chose out the fine cakes, and ate them themselves. And as for the bran one, they told her to take that to her Master. And she took it, and he broke it, and took out the files, and laid them away, and ate that cake and drank water, and was comforted.

And the people of the town wished that he should be killed. And he heard himself that it was said, "You shall be killed."

And he said to the soldiers, "When shall I be killed?"

And they told him, "Tomorrow."

And he said, "Call me my mother, and the chief man in the town, and all the townspeople, that I may take leave of them."

And they went and called them, and many people came together, and his mother and her slave.

And he asked them, "Are you all assembled?"

And they answered, "We are assembled."

And he said, "I want a horn, and cymbals, and an upato."

And they went and took them.

And he said, "I have an entertainment today, I want to take leave of you."

And they said to him, "Very well, go on, play."

And he said, "Let one take the horn, and one take the cymbals, and one take the upato."

And they said, "How shall we play them?"

And he taught them to play, and they played.

And he himself there, where he was inside, sang until the music was in full swing. Then he took a file and cut his fetters. When the music dropped, he too left off and sang, and when they played he cut his fetters.

And the people knew nothing of what was going on inside till the fetters were divided, and he cut the chains till they were divided. And still the people knew nothing of it through their delight in the music. When they eventually looked up, he had broken the door and come out to them outside. And they threw their instruments down to run away, without being quick enough, and he caught them and knocked their heads together and killed them. And he went outside the town, and took leave of his mother, "to see one another again."

And he went away into the forest, and stayed many days, harassing people as before, and killing people.

And they sent crafty men, and told them, "Go and make him your friend, so as to kill him." And they went in fear. And when they arrived they made a friendship with him. Till one day they said to him, "Sultan, let us entertain one another."

And Liongo answered them, "If I eat of an entertainment, what shall I give in return, I who am excessively poor?"

And they said to him, "Let us entertain one another with koma fruit."

And he asked them, "How shall we eat them?"

And they said, "One shall climb into the koma tree, and throw them down for us to eat. When we have done, let another climb up, till we have finished."

And he said to them "Very well."

And the first climbed up, and they ate. And the second climbed up, and they ate. And the third climbed up, and they ate. And they had plotted that when Liongo should climb up, "Let us shoot him with arrows there, up above."

But Liongo saw through it by his intelligence. So when all had finished they said to him, "Come, it is your turn."

And he said, "Very well." And he took his bow in his hand, and his arrows, and said, "I will strike the ripe fruit above, that we may eat in the midst." And he shot, and a bough was broken off, and he shot again, and a second was broken off, and he gave them a whole koma tree, and the ground was covered with fruit. And they ate.

And when they had done this, the men said among themselves, "He has seen through it. Now what are we to do?" And they said, "Let us go away." And they took leave of him, and said, "Liongo the chief, you have not been taken in, you are not a man, you have got out of it like a devil."

And they went away and gave their answer to their head-man there in the town, and said, "We could do nothing."

And they spoke together, "Who will be able to kill him?"

And they said, "Perhaps his nephew will." And they went and called him. And he came. And they said to him. "Go and ask your father what it is that will kill him. When you know, come and tell us, and when he is dead we will give you the kingdom."

And he answered them, "Very well."

And he went. When he arrived Liongo welcomed him and said, "What have you come to do?"

And he said, "I have come to see you."

And Liongo said, "I know that you have come to kill me, and they have deceived you."

And he asked him, "Father, what is it that can kill you?"

And he said, "A copper needle. If anyone stabs me in the navel, I die."

And he went away into the town, and answered them, and said, "It is a copper needle that will kill him." And they gave him a needle, and he went back to his father.

And when he saw him, his father sang, and said, "I, who am bad, am he that is good to you. Do me no evil. I that am bad, am he that is good to you." And he welcomed him, and he knew, "He is come to kill me."

And they stayed together for two days, till one day Liongo was asleep in the evening, and the boy stabbed him with the needle in the navel. And Liongo awoke through the pain, and took his bow and arrows and went to a place near the wells. And he knelt down, and put himself ready with his bow. And there he died.

So in the morning the people who came to draw water saw him, and they thought him alive, and went back running. And they gave out the news in the town, "No water is to be had today." Every one that went came back running. And many people set out and went, and as they arrived, when they saw him they came back, without being able to get near. For three days the people were in distress for water, not getting any.

And so they called his mother, and said to her, "Go and speak to your son, so that he may go away and we get water, or we will kill you."

And she went till she reached him. And his mother took hold of him to soothe him with songs, and he fell down. And his mother wept, for she knew her son was dead.

And she went to tell the townspeople that he was dead, and they went to look at him, and saw that he was dead, and buried him, and his grave is to be seen at Ozi to this day.

And then they seized that young man with the copper needle, and they killed him too, and did not give him the kingdom.

The Magician And The Sultan's Son

This story has been edited and adapted from George W. Bateman's Zanzibar Tales, Told by Natives of the East Coast of Africa, first published in 1901 by A. C. McClurg and Company in Chicago. The original stories were translated from the original Swahili and illustrated by Walter Bobbett.

There was once a Sultan who had three little sons, and no one seemed to be able to teach them anything, which greatly grieved both the Sultan and his wife.

One day a magician came to the Sultan and said, "If I take your three boys and teach them to read and write, and make great scholars of them, what will you give me?"

And the Sultan said, "I will give you half of my property."

"No," said the magician, "that won't do."

"I'll give you half of the towns I own."

"No, that will not satisfy me."

"What do you want, then?"

"When I have made them scholars and bring them back to you, choose two of them for yourself and give me the third, for I want to have a companion of my own."

"Agreed," said the Sultan.

So the magician took them away, and in a remarkably short time taught them to read, and to make letters, and made them quite good scholars. Then he took them back to the Sultan and said, "Here are the children. They are all equally good scholars. Choose."

So the Sultan took the two he preferred, and the magician went away with the third, whose name was Keejaanaa, to his own house, which was a very large one.

When they arrived, Mchaawee, the magician, gave the youth all the keys, saying, "Open whatever you wish to." Then he told him that he was his father, and that he was going away for a month.

When he was gone, Keejaanaa took the keys and went to examine the house. He opened one door, and saw a room full of liquid gold. He put his finger in, and the gold stuck to it, and, wipe and rub as he would, the gold would not come off, so he wrapped a piece of rag around it, and when his supposed father came home and saw the rag, and asked him what he had been doing to his finger, he was afraid to tell him the truth, so he said that he had cut it.

Not very long after, Mchaawee went away again, and the youth took the keys and continued his investigations.

The first room he opened was filled with the bones of goats, the next with sheep's bones, the next with the bones of oxen, the fourth with the bones of donkeys, the fifth with those of horses, the sixth contained men's skulls, and in the seventh was a live horse.

"Hello!" said the horse, "Where do you come from, you son of Adam?"

"This is my father's house," said Keejaanaa.

"Oh, indeed!" was the reply. "Well, you've got a pretty nice parent! Do you know that he occupies himself with eating people, and donkeys, and horses, and oxen and goats and everything he can lay his hands on? You and I are the only living things left."

This scared the youth pretty badly, and he faltered, "What are we to do?"

"What's your name?" said the horse.

"Keejaanaa."

"Well, I'm Faaraasee. Now, Keejaanaa, first of all, come and unfasten me."

The youth did so at once.

"Now, then, open the door of the room with the gold in it, and I will swallow it all. Then I'll go and wait for you under the big tree down the road a little way. When the magician comes home, he will say to you, 'Let us go for firewood.' You answer, 'I don't understand that work,' and he will go by himself. When he comes back, he will put a great big pot on the hook and will tell you to make a fire under it. Tell him you don't know how to make a fire, and he will make it himself.

"Then he will bring a large quantity of butter, and while it is getting hot he will put up a swing and say to you, 'Get up there, and I'll swing you.' But you tell him you never played at that game, and ask him to swing first, so that you may see how it is done. Then he will get up to show you and you must push him into the big pot, and then come to me as quickly as you can."

Then the horse went away.

Now, Mchaawee had invited some of his friends to a feast at his house that evening, so, returning home early, he said to Keejaanaa,

"Let us go for firewood," but the youth answered, "I don't understand that work." So he went by himself and brought the wood.

Then he hung up the big pot and said, "Light the fire," but the youth said, "I don't know how to do it." So the magician laid the wood under the pot and lighted it himself.

Then he said, "Put all that butter in the pot," but the youth answered, "I can't lift it. I'm not strong enough." So he put in the butter himself.

Next Mchaawee said, "Have you seen our country game?"

And Keejaanaa answered, "I think not."

"Well," said the magician, "let's play at it while the butter is getting hot."

So he tied up the swing and said to Keejaanaa, "Get up here, and learn the game."

But the youth said, "You get up first and show me. I'll learn quicker that way."

The magician got into the swing, and just as he got started Keejaanaa gave him a push right into the big pot, and as the butter was by this time boiling, it not only killed him, but cooked him also.

As soon as the youth had pushed the magician into the big pot, he ran as fast as he could to the big tree, where the horse was waiting for him.

"Come on," said Faaraasee, "jump on my back and let's be going."

So he mounted and they started off.

When the magician's guests arrived they looked everywhere for him, but, of course, could not find him. Then, after waiting a while, they began to be very hungry, so, looking around for something to eat, they saw that the stew in the big pot was done, and, saying to each other, "Let's begin, anyway," they started in and ate the entire contents of the pot. After they had finished, they searched for Mchaawee again, and finding lots of provisions in the house, they thought they would stay there until he came, but after they had waited a couple of days and eaten all the food in the place, they gave him up and returned to their homes.

Meanwhile Keejaanaa and the horse continued on their way until they had gone a great distance, and at last they stopped near a large town.

"Let us stay here," said the youth, "and build a house."

As Faaraasee was agreeable, they did so. The horse coughed up all the gold he had swallowed, with which they purchased slaves, and cattle, and everything they needed.

When the people of the town saw the beautiful new house and all the slaves, and cattle, and riches it contained, they went and told their Sultan, who at once made up his mind that the owner of such a place must be of sufficient importance to be visited and taken notice of, as an acquisition to the neighbourhoods.

So he called on Keejaanaa, and inquired who he was.

"Oh, I'm just an ordinary being, like other people."

"Are you a traveller?"

"Well, I have been, but I like this place, and think I'll settle down here."

"Why don't you come and walk in our town?"

"I should like to very much, but I need someone to show me around."

"Oh, I'll show you around," said the Sultan, eagerly, for he was quite taken with the young man.

After this Keejaanaa and the Sultan became great friends, and in the course of time the young man married the Sultan's daughter, and they had one son. They lived very happily together, and Keejaanaa loved Faaraasee as his own soul.

The Physician's Son And The King Of The Snakes

This story has been edited and adapted from George W. Bateman's Zanzibar Tales, Told by Natives of the East Coast of Africa, first published in 1901 by A. C. McClurg and Company in Chicago. The original stories were translated from the original Swahili and illustrated by Walter Bobbett.

Once there was a very learned physician, who died leaving his wife with a little baby boy, whom, when he was old enough, she named, according to his father's wish, Hasseeboo Kareem Ed Deen.

When the boy had been to school, and had learned to read, his mother sent him to a tailor, to learn his trade, but he could not learn it. Then he was sent to a silversmith, but he could not learn that trade either. After that he tried many trades, but could learn none of them. At last his mother said, "Well, stay at home for a while," and that seemed to suit him.

One day he asked his mother what his father's business had been, and she told him he was a very great physician.

"Where are his books?" he asked.

"Well, it's a long time since I saw them," replied his mother, "but I think they are behind there. Look and see."

So he hunted around a little and at last found them, but they were almost ruined by insects, and he gained little from them.

At last, four of the neighbours came to his mother and said, "Let your boy go along with us and cut wood in the forest." It was their business to cut wood, load it on donkeys, and sell it in the town for making fires.

"All right," said she, "tomorrow I'll buy him a donkey, and he can start fair with you."

So the next day Hasseeboo, with his donkey, went off with those four persons, and they worked very hard and made a lot of money that day. This continued for six days, but on the seventh day it rained heavily, and they had to get under the rocks to keep dry.

Now, Hasseeboo sat in a place by himself, and, having nothing else to do, he picked up a stone and began knocking on the ground with it. To his surprise the ground gave forth a hollow sound, and he called to his companions, saying, "There seems to be a hole under here."

Upon hearing him knock again, they decided to dig and see what the cause of the hollow sound was, and they had not gone very deep before they broke into a large pit, like a well, which was filled to the top with honey. They didn't do any firewood chopping after that, but devoted their entire attention to the collection and sale of the honey.

With a view to getting it all out as quickly as possible, they told Hasseeboo to go down into the pit and dip out the honey, while they put it in vessels and took it to town for sale. They worked for three days, making a great deal of money.

At last there was only a little honey left at the very bottom of the pit, and they told the boy to scrape that together while they went to get a rope to haul him out.

But instead of getting the rope, they decided to let him remain in the pit, and divide the money among themselves. So, when he had gathered the remainder of the honey together, and called for the rope, he received no answer, and after he had been alone in the pit for three days he became convinced that his companions had deserted him.

Then those four persons went to his mother and told her that they had become separated in the forest, that they had heard a lion roaring, and that they could find no trace of either her son or his donkey.

His mother, of course, cried very much, and the four neighbours pocketed her son's share of the money.

Hasseeboo, meanwhile passed the time walking about the pit, wondering what the end would be, eating scraps of honey, sleeping a little, and sitting down to think.

On the fourth day, while engaged in that last occupation, he saw a scorpion fall to the ground - a large one, too - and he killed it.

Then suddenly he thought to himself, "Where did that scorpion come from? There must be a hole somewhere. I'll search, anyhow."

So he searched around until he saw light through a tiny crack, and he took his knife and scooped and scooped, until he had made a hole big enough to pass through. Then he went out, and came upon a place he had never seen before.

Seeing a path, he followed it until he came to a very large house, the door of which was not fastened. So he went inside, and saw golden doors, with golden locks, and keys of pearl, and beautiful chairs inlaid with jewels and precious stones, and in a reception room he saw a couch covered with a splendid spread, upon which he lay down.

Presently he found himself being lifted off the couch and put in a chair, and heard someone saying, "Do not hurt him. Wake him gently," and on opening his eyes he found himself surrounded by numbers of snakes, one of them wearing beautiful royal colours.

"Hello!" he cried, "Who are you?"

"I am Sulta'nee Waa' Neeo'ka, king of the snakes, and this is my house. Who are you?"

"I am Hasseeboo Kareem Ed Deen."

"Where do you come from?"

"I don't know where I come from, or where I'm going."

"Well, don't bother yourself just now. Let's eat. I guess you are hungry, and I know I am."

Then the king gave orders, and some of the other snakes brought the finest fruits, and they ate and drank and conversed.

When the repast was ended, the king wanted to hear Hasseeboo's story, so he told him all that had happened, and then asked to hear the story of his host.

"Well," said the king of the snakes, "mine is rather a long story, but you shall hear it. A long time ago I left this place, to go and live in the mountains of Al Kaaf, for the change of air. One day I saw a stranger coming along, and I said to him, 'Where are you from?' and he said, 'I am wandering in the wilderness.' 'Whose son are you?' I asked. 'My name is Bolookeea. My father was a Sultan, and when he died I opened a small chest, inside of which I found a bag, which contained a small brass box. When I opened this I found some writing tied up in a woollen cloth, and it was all in praise of a prophet. He was described as such a good and wonderful man, that I longed to see him, but when I made inquiries concerning him I was told he was not yet born. Then I vowed I would wander until I should see him. So I left our town, and all my property, and I am wandering, but I have not yet seen that prophet.'

"Then I said to him, 'Where do you expect to find him, if he's not yet born? Perhaps if you had some serpent's water you might keep on living until you find him. But it's no use talking about that, for the serpent's water is too far away.'

"'Well,' he said, 'good-bye. I must wander on.' So I bade him farewell, and he went his way.

"Now, when that man had wandered until he reached Egypt, he met another man, who asked him, 'Who are you?'

"'I am Bolookeea. Who are you?'

"'My name is Al Faan. Where are you going?'

"'I have left my home, and my property, and I am seeking the prophet.

"'H'm!' said Al Faan, "I can tell you of a better occupation than looking for a man that is not born yet. Let us go and find the king of the snakes and get him to give us a charm medicine. Then we will go to King Solomon and get his rings, and we shall be able to make slaves of the genii and order them to do whatever we wish.'

"And Bolookeea said, 'I have seen the king of the snakes in the mountain of Al Kaaf.'

"'All right,' said Al Faan, 'let's go.'

"Now, Al Faan wanted the ring of Solomon so that he might become a great magician and control the genii and the birds, while all Bolookeea wanted was to see the great prophet.

"As they went along, Al Faan said to Bolookeea, 'Let us make a cage and entice the king of the snakes into it. Then we will shut the door and carry him off.'

"'All right,' said Bolookeea.

"So they made a cage, and put a cup of milk and a cup of wine in it as bait, and brought it to Al Kaaf, and I, like a fool, went in, drank up all the wine and became drunk. Then they fastened the door and took me away with them.

"When I came to my senses I found myself in the cage, with Bolookeea carrying me, and I said, 'The sons of Adam are no good. What do you want from me?'

"And they answered, 'We want some medicine to put on our feet, so that we may walk upon the water whenever it is necessary in the course of our journey.'

"'Well,' said I, 'go along.'

"We went on until we came to a place where there were a great number and variety of trees, and when those trees saw me, they said, 'I am medicine for this.' 'I am medicine for that.' 'I am medicine for the head.' 'I am medicine for the feet.' Presently one tree said, 'If anyone puts my medicine upon his feet he can walk on water.'

"When I told that to those men they said, 'That is what we want.' and they took a great deal of it.

"Then they took me back to the mountain and set me free, and we said good-bye and parted.

"When they left me, they went on their way until they reached the sea, when they put the medicine on their feet and walked over the water. They went on for many days, until they came near to the place of King Solomon, where they waited while Al Faan prepared his medicines.

"When they arrived at King Solomon's place, he was sleeping, and was being watched by genii, and his hand lay on his chest, with the ring on his finger.

"As Bolookeea drew near, one of the genii said to him 'Where are you going?'

"And he answered, 'I'm here with Al Faan. He's going to take that ring.'

"'Go back,' said the genie, "keep out of the way. That man is going to die.'

"When Al Faan had finished his preparations, he said to Bolookeea, 'Wait here for me.' Then he went forward to take the ring, when a great cry arose, and he was thrown by some unseen force a considerable distance.

"Picking himself up, and still believing in the power of his medicines, he approached the ring again, when a strong breath blew upon him and he was burnt to ashes in a moment.

"While Bolookeea was looking at all this, a voice said, 'Go on your way. This wretched being is dead.' So he returned, and when he got to the sea again he put the medicine upon his feet and passed over, and continued to wander for many years.

"One morning he saw a man sitting down, and said 'Good-morning,' to which the man replied. Then Bolookeea asked him, 'Who are you?'

"The man answered, 'My name is Jan Shah. Who are you?'

So Bolookeea told him who he was, and asked him to tell him his history. The man, who was weeping and smiling by turns, insisted upon hearing Bolookeea's story first. After he had heard it he said, 'Well, sit down, and I'll tell you my story from beginning to end. My name is Jan Shah, and my father is Tooeeghamus, a great Sultan. He used to go every day into the forest to shoot game. So one day I said to him, "Father, let me go with you into the forest today."

"But he said, "Stay at home. You are better there."

'Then I cried bitterly, and as I was his only child, whom he loved dearly, he couldn't stand my tears, so he said, "Very well, you shall go. Don't cry."

'Thus we went to the forest, and took many attendants with us, and when we reached the place we ate and drank, and then everyone set out to hunt.

'I and my seven slaves went on until we saw a beautiful gazelle, which we chased as far as the sea without capturing it. When the gazelle took to the water I and four of my slaves took a boat, the other three returning to my father, and we chased that gazelle until we lost sight of the shore, but we caught it and killed it. Just then a great wind began to blow, and we lost our way.

'When the other three slaves came to my father, he asked them, "Where is your Master?" and they told him about the gazelle and the boat. Then he cried, "My son is lost! My son is lost!" and returned to the town and mourned for me as one dead.

'After a time we came to an island, where there were a great many birds. We found fruit and water, we ate and drank, and at night we climbed into a tree and slept till morning.

'Then we rowed to a second island, and, seeing no one around, we gathered fruit, ate and drank, and climbed a tree as before. During the night we heard many savage beasts howling and roaring near us.

'In the morning we got away as soon as possible, and came to a third island. Looking around for food, we saw a tree full of fruit like red-streaked apples, but, as we were about to pick some, we heard a voice say, "Don't touch this tree. It belongs to the king." Toward night a number of monkeys came, who seemed much pleased to see us, and they brought us all the fruit we could eat.

'Presently I heard one of them say, "Let us make this man our Sultan." Then another one said, "What's the use? They'll all run away in the morning." But a third one said, "Not if we smash their boat." Sure enough, when we started to leave in the morning, our boat was broken in pieces. So there was nothing for it but to stay there and be entertained by the monkeys, who seemed to like us very much.

'One day, while strolling about, I came upon a great stone house, having an inscription on the door, which said, "When any man comes to this island, he will find it difficult to leave, because the monkeys desire to have a man for their king. If he looks for a way to escape, he will think there is none, but there is one outlet, which lies to the north. If you go in that direction you will come to a great plain, which is infested with lions, leopards, and snakes. You must fight all of them, and if you overcome them you can go forward. You will then come to another great plain, inhabited by ants as big as dogs, their teeth are like those of dogs, and they are very fierce. You must fight these also, and if you overcome them, the rest of the way is clear."

'I consulted with my attendants over this information, and we came to the conclusion that, as we could only die, anyhow, we might as well risk death to gain our freedom.

'As we all had weapons, we set forth, and when we came to the first plain we fought, and two of my slaves were killed. Then we went on to the second plain, fought again, and my other two slaves were killed, and I alone escaped.

'After that I wandered on for many days, living on whatever I could find, until at last I came to a town, where I stayed for some time, looking for employment but finding none.

'One day a man came up to me and said, "Are you looking for work?"

'"I am," said I.

'"Come with me, then," said he, and we went to his house.

'When we got there he produced a camel's skin, and said, "I shall put you in this skin, and a great bird will carry you to the top of yonder mountain. When he gets you there, he will tear this skin off you. You must then drive him away and push down the precious stones you will find there. When they are all down, I will get you down."

'So he put me in the skin, and the bird carried me to the top of the mountain and was about to eat me, when I jumped up, scared him away, and then pushed down many precious stones. Then I called out to the man to take me down, but he never answered me, and went away.

'I gave myself up for a dead man, but went wandering about, until at last, after passing many days in a great forest, I came to a house, all by itself. The old man who lived in it gave me food and drink, and I was revived.

'I remained there a long time, and that old man loved me as if I were his own son.

'"One day he went away, and giving me the keys, told me I could open the door of every room except one which he pointed out to me.

'Of course, when he was gone, this was the first door I opened. I saw a large garden, through which a stream flowed. Just then three birds came and alighted by the side of the stream. Immediately they changed into three most beautiful women. When they had finished bathing, they put on their clothes, and, as I stood watching them, they changed into birds again and flew away.

'I locked the door, and went away, but my appetite was gone, and I wandered about aimlessly. When the old man came back, he saw there was something wrong with me, and asked me what the matter was. Then I told him I had seen those beautiful maidens, that I loved one of them very much, and that if I could not marry her I should die.

'The old man told me I could not possibly have my wish. He said the three lovely beings were the daughters of the Sultan of the genii, and that their home was a journey of three years from where we then were.

'I told him I couldn't help that. He must get her for my wife, or I should die. At last he said, "Well, wait till they come again, then hide yourself and steal the clothes of the one you love so dearly."

'So I waited, and when they came again I stole the clothes of the youngest, whose name was Sayadaatee Shems.

'When they came out of the water, this one could not find her clothes. Then I stepped forward and said, "I have them."

'"Ah," she begged, "give them to me, their owner. I want to go away."

'But I said to her, "I love you very much. I want to marry you."

'"I want to go to my father," she replied.

'"You cannot go," said I.

'"Then her sisters flew away, and I took her into the house, where the old man married us. He told me not to give her those clothes I had taken, but to hide them, because if she ever got them she would fly away to her old home. So I dug a hole in the ground and buried them.

'But one day, when I was away from home, she dug them up and put them on, then, saying to the slave I had given her for an attendant, "When your Master returns tell him I have gone home. If he really loves me he will follow me," she flew away.

'When I came home they told me this, and I wandered, searching for her, many years. At last I came to a town where someone asked me, "Who are you?"

'I answered, "I am Jan Shah."

'"What was your father's name?"

'"Taaeeghamus."

'"Are you the man who married our mistress?"

'"Who is your mistress?"

'"Sayadaatee Shems."

'"I am he!" I cried with delight.

'They took me to their mistress, and she brought me to her father and told him I was her husband, and everybody was happy.

'Then we thought we should like to visit our old home, and her father's genii carried us there in three days. We stayed there a year and then returned, but in a short time my wife died. Her father tried to comfort me, and wanted me to marry another of his daughters, but I refused to be comforted, and have mourned to this day. That is my story.'

"Then Bolookeea went on his way, and wandered till he died."

Next Sultaanee Waa Neeoka said to Hasseeboo, "Now, when you go home you will do me injury."

Hasseeboo was very indignant at the idea, and said, "I could not be induced to do you an injury. Pray, send me home."

"I will send you home," said the king, "but I am sure that you will come back and kill me."

"Why, I dare not be so ungrateful," exclaimed Hasseeboo. "I swear I could not hurt you."

"Well," said the king of the snakes, "bear this in mind. When you go home, do not go to bathe where there are many people."

And he said, "I will remember."

So the king sent him home, and he went to his mother's house, and she was overjoyed to find that he was not dead.

Now, the Sultan of the town was very sick, and it was decided that the only thing that could cure him would be to kill the king of the snakes, boil him, and give the soup to the Sultan.

For a reason known only to himself, the Vizir had placed men at the public baths with this instruction, "If anyone who comes to bathe here has a mark on his stomach, seize him and bring him to me."

When Hasseeboo had been home three days he forgot the warning of Sultaanee Waa Neeoka, and went to bathe with the other people. All of a sudden he was seized by some soldiers, and brought before the Vizir, who said, "Take us to the home of the king of the snakes."

"I don't know where it is," said Hasseeboo.

"Tie him up," commanded the Vizir.

So they tied him up and beat him until his back was all raw, and being unable to stand the pain he cried, "Let up! I will show you the place."

So he led them to the house of the king of the snakes, who, when he saw him, said, "Didn't I tell you that you would come back to kill me?"

"How could I help it?" cried Hasseeboo. "Look at my back!"

"Who has beaten you so dreadfully?" asked the king.

"The Vizir."

"Then there's no hope for me. But you must carry me yourself."

As they went along, the king said to Hasseeboo, "When we get to your town I shall be killed and cooked. The first skimming the Vizir will offer to you, but don't drink it. Put it in a bottle and keep it. The second skimming you must drink, and you will become a great physician. The third skimming is the medicine that will cure your Sultan. When the Vizir asks you if you drank that first skimming say, 'I did.' Then produce the bottle containing the first, and say, 'This is the second, and it is for you.' The Vizir will take it, and as soon as he drinks it he will die, and both of us will have our revenge."

Everything happened as the king had said. The Vizir died, the Sultan recovered, and Hasseeboo was loved by all as a great physician.

Historical Notes

This section contains some brief biographical notes about the original collectors and their books featured in this collection. These notes have been adapted from those primarily on Wikipedia along with other supporting sources and notes.

Edward Steere

Edward Steere was born in 1828 and was an English Anglican colonial bishop in the 19th century.

He was educated at London University and ordained in 1850. After curacies in Devon and Lincolnshire, he joined William Tozer, then Bishop in Central Africa, on a mission to Nyasaland in 1863. He was appointed Bishop in Central Africa in 1874 and died on 26 August 1882.

Edward Steere spent several years in Zanzibar in the 1860's and 1870's. In 1873 he placed the foundation stone at Christ Church in Stone Town, Zanzibar. The cathedral was based on a vision that had inspired Steere, who then actively contributed to the design. The cathedral's unique concrete roof shaped in an unusual barrel vault was Steere's idea.

Edward Steere also worked with David Livingstone to abolish slavery in Zanzibar. David Livingstone's aides James Chuma and

Abdullah Susi were also part of an expedition lead by Steere, Chuma captaining the expedition, with both men acting as interpreters.

Steere was a considerable linguist and published works on several East African languages and dialects, including Shambala, Yao, Nyamwezi, and Makonde. He is especially known for his work on Swahili, publishing a *Handbook of Swahili* in 1870, and he also translated or revised the translation into Swahili of a large part of the Bible.

George W. Bateman

George W. Bateman was born in Essex, United Kingdom, in April 1840. He died in august 1940. He was the author of *Zanzibar Tales*, comprising folk stories that he translated from tales narrated to him by the locals of Zanzibar.

It is believed that some of these tales provided the inspiration for Disney stories such as Bambi and The Lion King.

Andrew Lang

Andrew Lang FBA was a Scottish poet, novelist, literary critic, and contributor to the field of anthropology. He is best known as a collector of folk and fairy tales. The Andrew Lang lectures at the University of St Andrews are named after him.

Lang was born on 31st March 1844 in Selkirk. He was the eldest of the eight children born to John Lang, the town clerk, and his wife Jane Plenderleath Sellar, who was the daughter of Patrick Sellar, factor to the first duke of Sutherland. On 17th April 1875, he married Leonora Blanche Alleyne, youngest daughter of C. T. Alleyne of Clifton and Barbados. She was (or should have been) variously credited as author, collaborator, or translator of Lang's Colour / Rainbow Fairy Books, which he edited.

He was educated at Selkirk Grammar School, Loretto School, and the Edinburgh Academy, as well as the University of St Andrews and Balliol College, Oxford, where he took a first class in the final classical schools in 1868, becoming a fellow and subsequently honorary fellow of Merton College. He soon made a reputation as one of the most able and versatile writers of the day as a journalist, poet, critic, and historian. In 1906, he was elected FBA.

He died of angina pectoris on 20th July 1912 at the Tor-na-Coille Hotel in Banchory, survived by his wife. He was buried in the cathedral precincts at St Andrews, where a monument can be visited in the south-east corner of the 19th century section.

Lang is now chiefly known for his publications on folklore, mythology, and religion. The earliest of his publications is *Custom and Myth* (1884). In *Myth, Ritual and Religion* (1887) he explained the "irrational" elements of mythology as survivals from more primitive forms. Lang's *Making of Religion* was heavily influenced by the 18th century idea of the "noble savage", in it, he maintained the existence of high spiritual ideas among so-called "savage" races, drawing parallels with the contemporary interest in occult phenomena in England.

His *Blue Fairy Book* (1889) was a beautifully produced and illustrated edition of fairy tales that has become a classic. This was followed by many other collections of fairy tales, collectively known as *Andrew Lang's Fairy Books*. In the preface of the *Lilac Fairy Book* he credits his wife with translating and transcribing most of the stories in the collections.

Lang was one of the founders of "psychical research" and his other writings on anthropology include *The Book of Dreams and Ghosts* (1897), *Magic and Religion* (1901) and *The Secret of the Totem*

(1905). He served as President of the Society for Psychical Research in 1911.

He collaborated with S. H. Butcher in a prose translation (1879) of Homer's *Odyssey*, and with E. Myers and Walter Leaf in a prose version (1883) of the *Iliad*, both still noted for their archaic but attractive style.

Lang's writings on Scottish history are characterised by a scholarly care for detail, a piquant literary style, and a gift for disentangling complicated questions. *The Mystery of Mary Stuart* (1901) was a consideration of the fresh light thrown on Mary, Queen of Scots, by the Lennox manuscripts in the University Library, Cambridge, approving of her and criticising her accusers.

Lang was active as a journalist in various ways, ranging from sparkling "leaders" for the Daily News to miscellaneous articles for the Morning Post, and for many years he was literary editor of Longman's Magazine.

About The Editor

I was born in 1962 into a predominantly sporting household – Dad being a good footballer, playing senior amateur and lower league professional football in England, as well as running a series of private businesses in partnership with mum, herself an accomplished and medal winning dancer.

I obtained a degree in History from Leeds University before wandering rather haphazardly into the emerging world of business computing in the late nineteen-eighties.

I followed a succession of amateur writing paths alongside my career in technology, including working as a freelance journalist and book reviewer, my one claim to fame being a by-line in a national newspaper in the UK, The Sunday people.

I also spent 10 years treading the boards, appearing all over the south of the UK in pantos and plays, in village halls and occasionally on the stage of a professional theatre or two.

Following the sporting theme I worked on live TV broadcasts for the BBC, ITV, TVNZ, EuroSport and others as a rugby "Stato", covering Heineken Cups, Six Nations, IRB World Sevens and IRB World Cups in the late '90's and early '00's.

You can find out more at: www.clivegilson.com

www.ingramcontent.com/pod-product-compliance
Lightning Source LLC
Chambersburg PA
CBHW030756190726
48285CB00003B/883